HISTORICAL FICTION

W9-CHC-324

G.F.S. LIBRARY

STEALING
MT. RUSHMORE

Daphne Kalmar

Feiwel and Friends
New York

A Feiwel and Friends Book
An imprint of Macmillan Publishing Group, LLC
120 Broadway, New York, NY 10271

Stealing Mt. Rushmore. Copyright © 2020 by Daphne Kalmar.
All rights reserved. Printed in the United States of America by
LSC Communications, Harrisonburg, Virginia.
Our books may be purchased in bulk for promotional, educational, or business use.
Please contact your local bookseller or the Macmillan Corporate and Premium
Sales Department at (800) 221-7945 ext. 5442 or by email at
MacmillanSpecialMarkets@macmillan.com.

Library of Congress Control Number: 2019940852
ISBN 978-1-250-15500-9 (hardcover) / ISBN 978-1-250-15499-6 (ebook)

Mt. Rushmore image used under license from Shutterstock.com

Book design by Katie Klimowicz
Feiwel and Friends logo designed by Filomena Tuosto

First edition, 2020
1 3 5 7 9 10 8 6 4 2
mackids.com

F
KAL
YA
(MG)

For Bridget, with love and gratitude

GERMANTOWN FRIENDS LIBRARY
ACC. NO._____1/21_____

Chapter 1

Boston Herald American, July 15, 1974
Moocher Missing Again

I sat at the kitchen table, reading the newspaper waiting for Dad to get home from work. Someone had stolen Moocher, the parrot, from the Stoneham Zoo again. I liked the look of him on the front page with his head tipped a little, staring at the camera in a friendly way.

Teddy, my six-year-old brother, sat next to me with his most precious possession—a sixty-four-color box of Crayola crayons with the built-in sharpener.

"Moocher got stolen again," I said.

We'd worried a lot about Moocher last year when he went missing the first time. Minnie, his mate for life, had been getting ready to lay some eggs, and she'd only take food from him. The first thief must have read about poor starving Minnie in the paper like we did. He must have felt rotten about what he'd done, since he turned Moocher over to a priest who gave him back to the zoo.

Teddy looked up from his Batman coloring book. "Is Minnie okay?"

"She's got two little chicks this time."

"How big are they?"

"Don't know, but they need Moocher to feed them."

Teddy's got a sad kind of face to begin with, but the hungry baby birds made it way worse.

"They'll find him," I said, and he got back to filling in Batman's cape.

Teddy believed I could fix any problem, like I was some superhero who could make everything okay. I was only thirteen years old with no superpowers and there wasn't much I could do about finding a stolen parrot. But I wasn't going to tell him that since he had enough to worry about.

The article in the paper said Moocher was really friendly. People could walk around the bird aviary, hold out handfuls of peanuts, and he'd land right on their arms for a snack. He was a super-rare kind of parrot, too, from some island in the Pacific Ocean—worth a thousand dollars. That's a lot of money for a bird. But even so, crooks should stick to stealing cash and gold and diamonds and keep their hands off live animals. Especially friendly parrots with baby chicks counting on them.

I moved my chair a little so I'd get the air from the fan full blast and stared at the Mt. Rushmore salt-and-pepper shakers sitting next to the napkin holder in the middle of the table. The presidents' faces on the shakers were kind of lumpy and pasty white. Salt came out of the top of the heads of George Washington and Thomas Jefferson, who were stuck together. The pepper came out of the Teddy Roosevelt and Abe Lincoln heads. Jefferson's chin had a few chips where the two shakers fit together like puzzle pieces.

I should have been on Mt. Rushmore but I wasn't. They're all men up there carved into that mountainside in South Dakota. Dad was counting on the orderly arrival, from left to right, of a baby George, a baby Thomas, a baby Teddy, and finally a baby Abe. But after George showed up I was born. A girl.

So I ended up being named after a near miss: Susan B. Anthony. She almost made it up on that mountain but Congress wouldn't spend the extra money. I think the money was a big fat excuse. Susan B. Anthony fought her whole life for a woman's right to vote, and Congress didn't want her up there giving the stink eye to those four presidents who got elected by a bunch of men.

Mom resisted the unlucky name of Susan since she had a cousin with that name who drowned in Boston

Harbor on New Year's Eve after she fell off a ferry at age seven. They never found the body. The *B* in Susan B. Anthony stands for Brownell, so everyone just called me Nell or Nellie. Not very presidential.

Teddy knelt on his chair, bent over his coloring book, a tight grip on his black crayon. He only had a stub left since he'd been working his way through the Batman coloring book for a week and it took a lot of black.

"It's two o'clock already," I said. "Eat your sandwich."

Teddy ignored me and kept coloring. He didn't like to stop in the middle of a section and he hardly ever colored outside the lines. If he slipped up, if Batman's mask or the skyscrapers of Gotham City didn't have crisp edges, he'd turn the page and start on a new picture.

"Eat your sandwich."

I reached over and made a grab for his box of crayons.

"Hey," he said, and gave me a look.

"Eat your sandwich."

"Okay."

Teddy closed his coloring book and slid the black crayon stub into its slot in the box. I pushed his peanut-butter-and-jelly sandwich over in front of him on a paper napkin. He started eating—one bite, chew, one swig of milk, swallow, repeat. It used to drive Mom crazy. "How about dripping some jelly on your shirt like a normal kid?" she'd say. He'd smile up at her like she'd paid him a compliment.

Dad gave me ten bucks a week to make sure Teddy ate something besides Popsicles, didn't stay in his pj's all day or get run over by a bus. Lousy pay, considering I had to take him with me everywhere I went all summer. But I didn't mind. I liked Teddy. And even if I didn't like him, no one else would hire me since I was too young. I guess if Mom hadn't run off I wouldn't have a job at all. A whole ton of stuff would be different if Mom hadn't run off.

Chapter 2

Like always, there was a headline on the front page that was going to upset Dad, who was a big fan of President Nixon—*More Impeachment Evidence Due*. The whole Watergate mess had been going on for years and it was getting worse and worse for the president. I started out reading the paper every day so I'd know in advance when Dad was gonna lose it. But now I was reading up on the hearings and trials of all of Nixon's aides because I'd gotten hooked on the whole story.

My habit of following the news about Watergate and the president was kind of like Mrs. O'Neill two houses down who was hooked on soap operas on TV. She watched what she called her "stories" every afternoon no matter what. One time last winter Mr. O'Neill came back from Manny's convenience store with a half gallon of milk and he'd forgotten his keys. Mrs. O'Neill didn't answer the door since *One Life to Live* was on and she thought it was the Jehovah's Witnesses or something and nothing got in the way of her stories. Mr. O'Neill banged on the door for a while, gave up, and came over to our house to get warm since it had started to snow. He could have frozen to death.

I knew all the names of the politicians and aides and prosecutors just like Mrs. O'Neill knew the names and histories of her soap opera characters. Except my people were real—Richard Nixon, John Ehrlichman, H. R. Haldeman, John Dean, Leon Jaworski, Sam Ervin, all of them. No one knew how it was going to end, just like on *The Guiding Light*.

I was reading the comics in the paper and Teddy was starting in on the second half of his sandwich when Dad came in the back door to the kitchen. He was tall but his shoulders sloped down, which made him look tired all the time, and most of the hair was gone on the top of his head.

"Hey, Nell. Hey, Teddy boy," he said.

He took off his work shoes, set them on the mat, put a paper sack in the fridge, and headed up the stairs. Right off, I could hear the shower going. Dad finished his shift as a short-order cook covered in a layer of grease—bacon grease, burger grease, fryer grease. Even though the exhaust fan in the kitchen at the Far Reach Diner could suck a pigeon out of midair, the grease still stuck. His hair, his skin, his clothes all stunk of it. When he got home and bent in for a kiss, Mom would push him away with both hands. She'd make a face like he was some kind of slimy creature who had crawled up out of the Charles River. And he'd smile at her anyway, just like Teddy. Every time.

Teddy was still eating. I read my horoscope for the day:

Taurus: Some complex situations indicated but none you cannot solve in your usual efficient manner. Don't be distracted by the frivolities of others.

I had no idea what *frivolities* were so I wasn't going to get distracted by any of them.

Mom's horoscope was pretty good but she would have laughed at it anyway. She was the one who got me started on them. Every morning, while I ate my cereal, she'd sit at the kitchen table, smoke a cigarette, drink her coffee, and in a fake-serious voice read our horoscopes out loud. Even though she made fun of it, I think she believed in them a little, like me.

Aries: You can mold this day as you choose. Others may inject their opinions with some force, but this need not affect your steady aim and direct approach to success—and with good will.

I had my doubts about her *success* since she wasn't ever big on *good will*. I had no idea where she was or what she was doing, so reading her horoscope was kind of like spying on her. I knew it was crazy since the horoscope was a bunch of hogwash, but if it was just a tiny bit true I had a peephole I could use to watch her from a distance.

Teddy was back to his coloring book and I was reading the details on page nine about Moocher when Dad stomped down the stairs in his boxers and T-shirt. He dumped his work clothes in the pile by the washing machine next to the back door.

"Hot one today, kids." He opened the freezer compartment of the fridge and glanced over his shoulder at the sink. "One of you didn't fill up the ice cube trays again. They're sitting in the sink."

"Sorry, Dad." It was probably Tom or George as usual so I don't know why *I* said sorry but I did.

He had both hands in the freezer. There was only one ice cube tray left for him to be tugging on. I'd seen it buried in the slow-moving glacier way in the back. No one had cooked the pork chops or defrosted the freezer since Mom left five months ago.

He stuck his head partway in.

"Damn it!"

Teddy looked up from his coloring book.

"What the hell?" Dad's voice was muffled by the frozen peas and pork chops.

"What?" asked Teddy.

I shook my head at him to keep him quiet. He put his black crayon in the box again and shut the lid. He was going to keep his crayons safe no matter what.

Dad gave a final tug and stepped back holding the ice cube tray. He threw it underhanded into the sink and it exploded. Ice cubes flew everywhere like a freak hailstorm happening right there in our kitchen.

"It's gone!" Dad yelled.

He pulled open the top drawer next to the fridge and lifted out a big, pointy knife. Holding on to it with a grip a psycho uses in a horror movie, he started to chip away at the ice in the freezer. Every time he stabbed at the glacier the screeching, twisty, *thunk* made me cringe. Teddy and I stayed real still in our seats. Ice chips, like shards of glass, covered the floor around us.

Dad set the knife on the counter and stuck both his hands in the freezer. He yanked out a blue Maxwell House coffee can, held it upside down, and shook it. The duct tape that had sealed it shut was slit open and the plastic lid flapped up and down. He slammed the freezer door shut, turned, and threw the coffee can against the wall.

"Damn her." He didn't yell it but there was a shudder in his voice that made my stomach clutch.

I squeezed up against the back of my chair, tried to keep clear. Teddy scrambled to his feet and moved close to me, our shoulders touching. I put my arm around him, could feel him trembling. I wasn't scared of my dad but he was taking up a lot of space.

He stormed out of the kitchen, fists clenched, mumbling, "Damn her," over and over. We followed him at a distance and stopped by the stairs. Teddy held on to my shirt like he used to do when he was really little.

Dad threw the front door open and stood on the stoop in his boxers and white T-shirt. "Where the hell is it, Connie?" he hollered. "Running off wasn't bad enough? You had to steal Mt. Rushmore?"

Through the front window, across the street, I could see Mrs. Longmire pull her curtains back. Nosy old witch ought to mind her own business.

Dad stood on the stoop in his bare feet, the varicose veins in his legs bulging and purple from standing all day in the kitchen at the Far Reach for years and years. After a minute, he just standing there, his shoulders and head sagged like someone had popped him with a pin. All the anger drained out of him and floated down the street.

I bit my lower lip. I knew what was going to happen next and my horoscope got it all wrong. I wasn't going to be able to solve this *complex situation in my usual efficient manner*. I'd need a miracle and maybe some *frivolities* once I found out what the heck they were.

Chapter 3

My brother Tom, who's ten, came up from the basement, stopped short, and stared at Dad, standing in his T-shirt and boxers on the stoop.

"What happened?" he asked in a loud whisper.

"Mt. Rushmore's gone," I said, still watching Dad. "All five hundred bucks."

Teddy let go of my shirt, went and got the coffee can and carried it into the living room.

"Someone cut it open," he said, trying to fit the lid back on.

"Road trip's off, then," said Tom, plopping down on the couch.

Teddy and I walked over and sat next to him.

Dad came inside. Didn't look at us.

"Road trip's dead." His voice was flat, his back turned. He closed the front door. I kind of wished he'd slammed it, since I was doubly sure now from his voice and his face that he'd gone all sad like before. At least when he was mad he was there, solid and loud, right in front of me.

When he thumped up the stairs I wasn't sure if he was going to come back down again. Before Mom left, the Mt. Rushmore trip was all he talked about. When the second week of August rolled around we were all gonna pile into his Dodge Dart with the slant-six engine that would never quit, and hit the road. Mom wasn't too thrilled. "Sleeping in a leaky tent, getting eaten alive by mosquitoes. Not exactly Disneyland, is it?" she said, but she'd smiled a little. She knew how much he was counting on that trip. Which made what she'd done even worse.

Mom had deep-sixed *my* big adventure, too. I'd only ever set foot in two states: Massachusetts, where I'd been stuck my whole entire life, and Rhode Island, where, when I was five, we'd stayed in a motel by the beach. That was before I learned how to swim at the YMCA on Mass. Ave., so I was only allowed to go into the ocean up to my knees.

We were going to drive through tons of states on the way to South Dakota, and I'd planned to collect postcards and ticket stubs and other stuff along the way so I could put them in the photo album I had with plastic sheets that held everything straight.

Tom picked up a Green Hornet comic book off the coffee table and pretended to read.

"Dad thinks she stole it," I said.

"Mom?"

"Yeah." I kicked the table leg.

"What'd Mom do?" asked Teddy, sitting in between us on the couch, still holding the coffee can.

"She stole the money for our road trip to Mt. Rushmore," I said, trying to keep my voice normal around Teddy even though it should have been a growl, a hiss that would have scared off a pack of lions.

Dad had saved for two years. Back in January we'd all watched when he sealed up that coffee can with duct tape. "There it is, kiddos. Five hundred smackers," he'd said, holding it up high. "It's gonna be a great summer." We all clapped when he shoved the can in the back of the freezer. Well, not George, my fifteen-year-old brother. He just gave us all a look like we were the most pathetic family on the planet. And not Mom, either. She didn't clap.

"Why'd she steal it?" said Teddy.

"Guess she needed running-away money," I said.

"Yeah," said Tom, throwing the comic book down

15

on the coffee table. "And now it's no tents, no Rocky Mountains, no campfires, no nothin'."

"No so mores?" said Teddy, his face scrunching up.

"No s'mores," I said.

"I've been thinking a lot about the so mores," said Teddy.

There wasn't a sound from upstairs. Dad had climbed into bed. He'd gotten crazy angry and lost hold of it, let it turn into sad—a deep-end-of-the-swimming-pool kind of sad, where a person could drown.

Mt. Rushmore was more than a carving in a mountain to Dad. "Boot camp out west was over," he'd said. "I was just out of high school, going off to war. Scared silly. But then I saw it—like walking into a cathedral or something, set up against that blue sky they've got out west, nothing like ours. I looked up at those great presidents and fell in love with America. You've gotta see it, kids."

We sat there lined up on the couch, not moving. The silence made me dizzy—like someone had swiped the safety net while I teetered back and forth on a tightrope way off the ground. Teddy held on to the Maxwell House coffee can like it was a life preserver or something. Dad was gone even though he was right upstairs. I wanted to drag him back but I knew I couldn't. I'd tried that last time. We were on our own.

Moms weren't supposed to steal people's dreams. They weren't supposed to walk out the door and not come back, either. I reminded myself to breathe and stopped chewing my lip since it was just piling on the hurt.

Teddy looked up at me. "Is Mom gonna come home now?"

"What?" I said, staring at him.

"To bring the money?"

"No," said Tom. "She's not."

I scrubbed Teddy's head. "It's gonna be okay." It was a lie, but he was just a little kid.

The back door banged open. I knew right off it was George, since he always banged through doors. If he didn't make enough noise banging into the house he'd kick the door shut behind him. He came into the living room and looked us up and down.

"Why're you three clowns sitting there like sad little puppies?" He laughed and wiped his hands on his jeans. He bussed tables and washed dishes at the Far Reach, so he was even greasier than Dad.

I didn't say a word. Neither did Tom or Teddy. He just got meaner if one of us gave it back to him. George shook his head and kicked off his sneakers. "Like I give a crap anyway," he said, and climbed the stairs.

George didn't care about anything or anyone except

the big wad of cash he'd been saving for the car he was going to buy as soon as he turned sixteen in October and got his license. It wouldn't have been much fun sitting next to him all the way to South Dakota. But I didn't care, I still wanted to see that mountain Dad had talked about my whole entire life and Mom had flat-out stolen it.

Tom got up first. "Gotta work on my Huey," he said.

"Can I watch?" said Teddy.

"Yeah."

Teddy handed me the coffee can like I might need it or something and they both disappeared down the basement stairs. Tom had set up a couple of old folding tables for his model building in a corner down there. He spent every last dime he earned from his paper route on the latest model jet fighter or World War I fighter plane. He'd been working on his Huey Hog helicopter for a couple of weeks.

It had helped to have Tom and Teddy sitting right there, next to me on the couch. With them gone the house was too quiet. I pulled my bare feet up on the cushion and hugged my knees. Dad always disappeared upstairs when he lost his temper—when the washing machine broke or when Tom and his best friend, Carlos, pitched a baseball through the back window or when Mom got going complaining about her life.

When he'd walk up the stairs Mom would make some

crack. "Go on, hide under the covers. Have a good sulk." I didn't think he was sulking. I figured he was staying away from everyone so he wouldn't get more angry, but the staying away let the sadness creep in like darkness slips under a bedroom door when the lights in the hall go out.

Some kids I know got introduced to their dad's belt if they stepped out of line. I'd rather have a dad who crawled under the covers. And up until Mom walked out, Dad had always gotten up the next day and gone to work. Always. Mom said he barely made it to the hospital when each of us kids was born. "He thought slopping the hogs at that diner was more important than being there by my side while I was screaming bloody murder giving birth to you all." Considering Mom's big mouth I'm surprised the doctors and nurses had stuck around to make sure we all came out headfirst.

But when she left, he didn't get up and go to work. Dad stayed in bed for a whole week, except when he got up to pee, or eat something standing in the kitchen, or take a shower a couple of times. He didn't say a word, acted like the four of us were invisible.

I sat there on the couch hugging my knees and wondered if this going to bed was like the Mom-running-off going to bed. Or maybe worse. Dad didn't even have Mt. Rushmore anymore to give him some hope.

I rocked a little and shut my eyes to stop thinking.

The shower started upstairs. George was getting cleaned up. The muggy heat and Dad in bed had given me a stomachache. I got up and walked into the kitchen. If Mom were there standing by the sink, she'd make some crack about the disappearance of Mt. Rushmore. "Not playing with a full deck if you misplace a mountain." She almost always made things worse. But at least she'd be standing there. I hated her for stealing the money.

But I wanted her back.

Chapter 4

Dad was in bed and the boys were in the basement. I yanked the phone off the receiver on the wall and called Maya. Her mom, Mrs. Machado, answered.

"Hi, is she there?"

"Hi, dear." I heard the phone plunk down on the table. "Maya, it's Nellie!" It took forever.

"Yeah?" Maya said.

"Hey, it's me. Come over."

"Can't. Gotta stock shelves."

"Come on," I said. "Bad stuff's happening over here."

"What?"

"Come over."

"Okay. Give me half an hour."

I got the mop and cleaned up most of the melted ice on the kitchen floor, filled the ice cube trays and set them in the freezer. Twenty-five minutes to go. I sat at the table and opened up Nancy Drew #7. Two weeks ago Mrs. O'Neill showed up at our door and gave me a box filled with thirty-eight Nancy Drew mysteries. They'd belonged to her daughter, Fiona, who'd gotten married and moved to Melrose. "You'll get some use out of them," she said. "Spent all her babysitting money on those books. Read them over and over till the next one came out."

So far I'd read the first six books in the series and Maya had started to read them, too. We'd agreed that Nancy's sports car was the coolest. She was always smarter than the bad guys and incredibly brave running down dark alleys and charging into haunted houses. I had thirty-two books left so I didn't have to worry about running out. And there were plenty more at the library since a new one came out every year. Maya'd seen the latest—*The Mystery of the Glowing Eye*, #51. Sounded creepy in a good way.

After thirty minutes I set #7 down on the kitchen table. Maya was late again. Like always. And Teddy was going to get bored watching Tom glue plastic parts together and end up wandering around the house all alone.

I opened the basement door and yelled down the stairs, "Teddy, wanna go for a walk?"

"Okay," he said.

"Pee. And get your cap."

We were all ready to go and Maya still hadn't shown up. It was only a five-minute walk from the Machados' apartment but she was probably changing her clothes for the tenth time that day. When she walked in I could tell I was right.

"What's the emergency?" she asked, sitting down at the table. Her makeup was all fresh, enough blue eye shadow to paint our house, and her dark hair was tied up in a perfect ponytail. She had on blue shorts and a sleeveless blouse that looked like she'd just ironed it.

"Let's go for a walk and I'll fill you in," I said.

Right when we stood up to go George slammed into the kitchen.

"Hello, Maya," he said, grinning.

She ignored him. He'd hardly noticed her before she grew boobs and started wearing her sisters' makeup.

"Let's go," I said.

George grabbed for Teddy's cap and he ducked.

"Going out with your girlfriends, squirt?" he said.

"Cut it out," I said.

On the street I could breathe better with Maya right next to me. Teddy ran ahead. He'd stop to dig a soda pop pull tab out of a crack in the pavement or in the dirt around one of the beat-up trees planted along the sidewalk. He'd shove it in his pocket and move on, searching for more. Teddy had a huge glass pickle jar from the Far Reach on his bureau almost filled up with his collection. It was kind of disgusting, considering all the slobber and dog poop and yuck those pull tabs were covered with.

Maya nudged my shoulder. "So?"

"It's my mom."

"She call?"

"No."

A carload of teenage boys drove by real slow. They all hooted at us, their arms hanging out the windows banging on the car doors. Well, they weren't hooting at me, just Maya, who got this all the time with her makeup and short shorts that made her look sixteen.

If turning sixteen meant I'd get all those stares and whistles, I planned on staying thirteen forever. Maya didn't flinch—she kept walking like they weren't even there.

"Dad dug around in the freezer," I said. "Someone swiped the money for our Mt. Rushmore trip."

"Your mom?"

"Who else?"

Maya whistled. She was an excellent whistler.

"Dad went nuts. Now he's gone to bed."

"Like last time?"

"Not sure."

We kept walking and caught up with Teddy, who was waiting for us at the corner.

"Someone stole Moocher again, too," I said.

"The parrot?"

I caught hold of Teddy's hand and we crossed the street.

"Minnie has two baby chicks," said Teddy.

"What kind of creep steals a bird?" said Maya.

"They're gonna find him for sure," said Teddy.

I gave Maya a quick nod.

"You bet they are, kiddo," she said.

We got across the street and Teddy ran ahead. John and Eddie from two blocks over came tearing down the sidewalk on their skateboards, dodged Teddy, headed straight for us, and swerved to miss us at the last minute, laughing their heads off.

"Dirt wads," yelled Maya.

They laughed harder, proving they *were* dirt wads. A month ago the two of them almost ran down Mrs. Mendez when she was getting out of her car—scared her half to death.

"I'm not so sure he's getting out of bed this time," I said.

Saying it out loud made it too real. I wanted to unsay

it, like that would fill the coffee can back up with money and fix everything.

"He will." Maya touched my shoulder and smiled. I knew she was saying it to make me feel better, like how she'd told Teddy that Moocher was going to get rescued. But it still made me believe it just a little.

"Mom stole the trip from *me,* too—New York, Pennsylvania, Ohio, Indiana, Illinois, Michigan, Minnesota, *and* South Dakota."

"Sucks," said Maya. "All your new states."

We caught up with Teddy at the next intersection.

"Maybe I could come up with the money," I said, and laughed. "I've got three weeks."

"Five hundred bucks," said Maya. "What're you gonna do, rob a bank?"

Teddy turned and studied my face, waiting for an answer.

"No, Teddy, I'm not gonna rob a bank," I said.

He nodded and ran ahead.

"What are you gonna do?" Maya asked.

I swallowed. A beer truck rumbled by and kicked up the dirt on the road. Sweat trickled down my back.

"I don't know," I said. "But I've gotta do something."

Chapter 5

When we got to Crowley Street, Teddy stopped at the chain-link fence around Russell Elementary to dig up a pull tab. He started there in kindergarten this past year, the year Maya and me moved on to junior high. It was an old brick building with a flagpole out front. I could see the three tall windows of my fifth-grade classroom on the second floor. They used to rattle when the wind blew. If I'd had a choice I would have stayed in that class forever with Mrs. Caputo, my favorite teacher of all time, Maya at her desk right next to mine, and my crabby mom still living in our house on Carlisle Street.

The playground was empty.

"Quick game?" I said.

Maya gave me a raised-eyebrows "You're kidding" look. We hadn't played hopscotch in two whole years.

"Come on," I said.

She eyed the playground and grinned.

Teddy came up to us. "Why're we stopping?"

"We're gonna play hopscotch, kiddo," said Maya.

We walked around looking for decent throwing stones while Teddy went back to his search for pull tabs. The hopscotch court was painted in white on the hard-top next to the monkey bars, swings, and slide. Teddy sat on a swing to watch. Maya won Rock, Paper, Scissors two out of three, so she went first. She got to the fourth square and missed her throw.

"Lousy marker. Rolled halfway to Kansas," she said, sounding disgusted.

"Lousy throw," I said.

"It was a perfect throw." She gave me a fake scowl. I laughed because we were playing hopscotch and Maya's shirt had a smudge of dirt on it, her ponytail was coming loose, and she didn't care.

When we started playing hopscotch back in first grade, the painted courts were too big for our short legs, and the older kids hogged them anyway. We swiped chalk from the classroom blackboard and drew our own smaller court over by the parking lot.

Other first graders played, too, sometimes, but Maya and me were in love with the game and kept it up all through elementary school. We played every recess and before and after school unless there was snow on the ground.

I threw my stone marker, jumped over it, landed on my right foot, hopped, made a two-footed landing on the first cross, hopped, and landed two footed on the second cross. It all came back, like being in a time machine from *The Twilight Zone,* when in a flash the soldier was back home, eight years old, sitting at the table eating dinner with his family. I did a perfect jump and turn, hop, two-foot landing, hop, hop, picked up my stone, and leaped to safety.

Gripping my marker stone I smiled at Maya and she smiled back. Right then we were ten years old again playing our favorite game. Right then she was the best friend in the universe.

Teddy twirled around on the wooden seat of his swing once in a while, but mostly watched. We played three games and ended up on the swings ourselves, all sweaty and hot.

"That was great," said Maya.

I wanted to give her a big hug but I didn't. "Your shirt's all wrinkled."

"Who cares?" she said, and pushed off the ground, kicking her feet up in the air as she swung in a giant arc.

The hopscotch happiness drained away as we got closer to my house with Dad upstairs in bed.

Maya stopped and looked at me hard. Teddy waited at the intersection at the end of the block.

"You okay?" she asked.

"Sort of." I swallowed.

"Maybe it's not the same. Maybe he's outside right now washing his car."

"Maybe."

Maya looked at her watch. "Call me later. Gotta get home. Mom only gave me an hour."

Mrs. Machado was seriously strict. Maya wasn't allowed to do much of anything on her own. Even coming over to my house she had time limits. Her mom never liked my mom much and was never very happy with Maya coming over. She always phoned first to make sure Mom was around to supervise, which was pretty funny. Mom was never big on supervision. She liked it best when we were all running around outside. And it didn't matter where. With Mom gone Mrs. Machado felt sorry for me, so she let Maya come over but got even stricter about time limits.

"See ya," I said.

Maya waved and crossed the street.

When we got to our block Teddy ran on ahead. I took a long gulp of humid air. Mom stealing the money for our trip was a joke since she was a part-time store detective at Woolworths in Central Square. Every day she'd come home with stories about lowlifes who stole stuff. She'd walk across the living room all bowlegged. "This old lady got all the way to the door with a tape recorder between her knobby knees under her skirt." She'd laugh about the kids stuffing comic books down their pants. "The manager put them right back on the rack after they'd been down there. I ought to sic the health department on him."

Mom wore regular clothes to blend in and wandered the aisles in the store like any old customer. Skinny and short, no one would ever suspect she was watching them, that she knew all the tricks of the trade. And she was coldhearted when she caught them. "Heard a grade-A sob story today," she'd say, and laugh. Mom was cold-hearted when she stole our big trip out West, too. And she didn't just swipe a pair of sunglasses or a Milky Way. She stole Dad's dream. And as far as I could tell it was the only one he had.

Teddy was sitting on the stoop waiting for me. I pulled my house key out of my pocket. I don't think either one of us wanted to go inside. When we walked into the living room it was dead quiet. The TV was off, Dad's recliner with the ketchup stain on the arm was empty. In the kitchen there was a note on the fridge.

Chapter 6

The note was in Dad's handwriting, in crayon—blue crayon.

DINNER IN FRIDGE

That was it. He didn't go in for long notes. But this one didn't cut the mustard. Not when he took a nutter, attacked an innocent freezer with a knife, and yelled at the top of his lungs standing on the stoop in his underwear. I already knew where our dinner was. I'd been right there when he put the bag from the Far Reach in the fridge like always. He could have said "Sorry" or "Love, Dad" or "See you in the morning." But he didn't.

Teddy sat at the table holding his broken blue-violet

crayon. The look on his face was like he was at a funeral or something. He stared at that crayon Dad had murdered, his eyes all shiny with tears. I ripped the note up, threw it in the trash, and got the Scotch tape out of the bowl on the counter.

"Hold it together," I said.

Teddy fussed with the two pieces until he had the writing lined up on the paper band and I wound a piece of tape around it. He laid his crayon gently on the table like it needed to recover from surgery. It was all just too sad.

"How about a swim?" I said.

"Okay."

While he was upstairs changing into his swimsuit I went into the backyard, untangled the hose, and filled the plastic kiddie pool. Teddy should have been swimming in a real pool all summer at the YMCA kiddie camp on Mass. Ave. But without Mom's paycheck Dad couldn't swing it, even for a couple of weeks.

Money was tight. A few months ago the electric bill showed up in a bright yellow envelope. "Lights Out Yellow," Dad called it. He'd been late paying the bill and had thirty days to get caught up or we'd have no electricity. But even if Boston Edison shut our power off he would have never, ever touched the five hundred bucks in the freezer. That Maxwell House coffee can would have been safe, sitting in a puddle in the dead freezer next to a package of stinking pork chops.

Teddy came outside. His swim trunks from last year were too tight around his middle and his arms and legs were so skinny he looked like he might break. He poked his foot in the water, stepped in, counted to three, and sat down.

"It's cold!" he said, and splashed around in a circle on his butt. I dragged a lawn chair over and sat down with my feet in the water. There was a little breeze and the trees in the backyard gave us some shade.

"Why's water cold?" asked Teddy.

"You mean why does it cool you off?"

"Yeah."

"Don't know. Something about evaporation."

"What's evapolution?"

We talked as Teddy splashed around but we both got quiet after a while. Teddy kind of mumbled to himself while he floated leaves and sticks on the surface and sunk them with pebbles. I didn't have to watch him since he'd have to work hard to drown.

Back in the kitchen I sat at the table in front of the fan. Tom was off with Carlos somewhere and who knew where George was. I got a glass of Kool-Aid and read the last twenty pages of Nancy Drew #7. Nancy chased a dangerous criminal down a long dark driveway and of course he confessed. The innocent guy got out of jail. She always wrapped everything up all neat and tidy at the end, which isn't how the real world works. But I didn't care. Knowing everything was going to be okay was why I liked the books in the first place.

At six o'clock I set the oven on low and pulled the paper sack from the Far Reach out of the fridge. It was Monday so it must be meat loaf. Ever since Mom left we'd been eating Far Reach food most nights. Dad had made a deal with Lou, the owner, to put in overtime in exchange for takeout dinners. He stuck to a schedule like he did for everything.

THURSDAY: LASAGNA
FRIDAY: FISH STICKS
SATURDAY: CHICKEN A LA KING
SUNDAY: MAC AND CHEESE
MONDAY: MEAT LOAF

We got a break from the Far Reach menu on Tuesdays and Wednesdays, Dad's days off, when I was stuck heating up TV dinners or franks and beans for everyone. We ate better now that Mom wasn't around. She was a lousy cook. Burned the chicken or chops. Served up soggy mashed potatoes and mushy peas. I had helped—stirring and peeling and cleaning up but it wasn't easy being in the kitchen with her. She got real crabby while she burned our dinner. "This is my life— potato buds," she'd yell, holding up the box. "How did this damn sink fill up with dirty dishes again?" "OUT! Just get out of my way!"

I stopped for a minute. Stood and listened. Dad still hadn't come downstairs but I'd heard the toilet flush while I was reading so I knew he was still up there. I slipped the pie tins filled with meat loaf and mashed potatoes into the oven on a cookie sheet. Some music would have helped with the quiet but Mom had stolen that, too.

There was a big empty space on the counter where the record player used to sit along with a stack of records. Bob Dylan, the Beatles, James Taylor, the Supremes, Joni Mitchell—all the music Mom loved and Dad hated. "You can shut that off now," he'd say when he got home. She'd turn the music off but look at me and roll her eyes. I'd grin back like we were on the same side. *The same side.* That's a laugh.

When he wasn't home, Mom used to play those records until they might wear out and sometimes we'd dance—me, Teddy, Mom, and even Tom, right there in the kitchen. And we'd sing, too. When the last song on the record ended and we were done dancing she'd get mean again. "Out of here, all of you, I've got to make your damn dinner." But Mom couldn't deny that we danced sometimes. That we were happy while the music played and she forgot how angry she was being stuck with four kids in a run-down house in Somerville, Massachusetts.

The music had been gone for five months. I played the radio sometimes but it wasn't the same. I'd been saving my pay from Dad for watching Teddy to buy a real stereo and a pile of records so I could get it back. But that wasn't going to happen anytime soon. I'd have to use the seventy-eight dollars I'd saved so far to buy back Mt. Rushmore. Mom was dancing all by herself now.

"Screw you," I said.

I half filled a saucepan with water and banged it down on the stove. Teddy came inside and dried himself off with the beach towel hanging on the back door. He kneeled on his chair at the table and opened his coloring book to a new picture.

"What color are windows?" he asked.

I studied the picture of Batman and Robin hanging on wires attached to their belts climbing the outside of a skyscraper.

"Make them rainbow colors," I said.

"Okay," he said, and pulled the pink crayon out of the box. George banged in through the back door.

"Hey, squirt," he said.

Teddy looked up from his coloring book but didn't answer. I yanked a box of frozen peas out of the freezer.

I still did a double take when I noticed George. He must've grown half a foot in the last year and his face had gotten handsome. Maya said it was a waste that such a pig was so dreamy looking.

"Dad's upstairs," I said. "In bed, again."

"Yeah?" he said.

"Mom stole the money for our trip."

"So? What do I care?"

I ignored his nastiness. "We've got to get to Mt. Rushmore."

He didn't answer me, grabbed a handful of Oreos out of the package on the counter.

"I'm gonna try to pull the money together," I said.

"Not getting any from me. Dad already takes twenty bucks a week out of my paycheck."

"You live here. You eat the food."

"Really hit the jackpot, didn't I?"

"I'm gonna get the money."

"Yeah? That'll be a neat trick."

He sat across from Teddy and started messing with his crayon box. Teddy shrunk down in his chair and looked over at me for help. George picked up the taped blue-violet crayon and examined it.

"Have a little accident?" he said, making a phony sad face.

Teddy reached for his crayon and George held it up over his head.

"Quit it," I said.

George laughed and handed Teddy the crayon. "Quit what?"

"You've got buckets of money."

"Listen," he said. "I don't give a damn about Dad or that mountain."

"We were gonna have so mores," said Teddy, who'd moved his box of crayons over to his side of the table for safekeeping.

George pushed his chair back and got up.

"You're a selfish pig," I said, spitting a little on the *pig* part.

"Yeah? She doesn't think so. Hung up three times when Dad answered. Only wanted to talk to me, *the selfish pig*."

I stared at George. Teddy stopped coloring and looked up.

"Mom?" I said.

"Yeah. Said she was broke. Asked for the Rushmore money. I took it. Got a money order at the post office, and mailed it to her."

"You talked to Mom?"

He just stood there.

"You stole the money? For *her*?"

I wanted to punch him right in that pretty face of his. He'd talked to Mom. Knew she wasn't dead in an alley somewhere. And he hadn't told me or Dad or anyone. Just let us worry and wonder and feel rotten for wanting to yell at her when she might be dead.

"When?"

"Couple of months ago." He said it all casual like it wasn't a big shocker or anything.

"Mommy's coming home?" said Teddy, his face wide open with happiness.

"Not a chance." George turned and banged out the back door.

I went after him.

"Hey!"

He turned. "What do you want?"

"You stole Dad's money!"

"Get lost." He headed down the driveway.

I followed him, yelling, "It wasn't hers!"

Glenn was parked by the curb in his old Chevy, his eight track blasting Led Zeppelin out the open windows.

"It was Dad's!" I yelled, as George got in the car.

They drove off down the street and I stood there, my fists clenched. I wanted to get hold of Tom's baseball bat and smash every window in every parked car on the street. I wanted to swing that bat like the great left fielder, Carl Yastrzemski, and take George's head off.

"Is he coming back?" said Teddy in a small voice behind me.

I turned. He was standing on the curb in his bathing suit holding his blue-violet crayon in his right hand, crying so hard he was gulping for air, his skinny shoulders heaving. I kneeled down and put my arms around him. He crawled up onto me and I tipped over. I sat up on the sidewalk and pulled him into my lap and let him cry. I hugged him tight because he needed it and I did, too.

Chapter 7

Teddy and I walked back to the house, past Dad's
Dodge Dart and up the stairs to the back door.
He climbed into his chair and set his blue-violet
crayon on the table.

"George's coming back," I said. "And when he does
I'm gonna let him have it."

"What?" Teddy looked up at me all red-eyed with
snot on his face.

I pulled a Kleenex out of the box on the counter and
handed it to him.

"Nothing. Blow your nose, snot face."

He smiled. "Okay."

It was boiling hot in the kitchen with the oven on.
I grabbed the box of frozen peas off the counter and

ripped it open. Half of them sprayed all over the kitchen floor.

"That's just perfect," I said.

Teddy giggled. I laughed and grabbed the broom.

I dumped what was left of the peas in the pot and turned the burner on. I wanted to call Maya and tell her about George but Teddy was right there and I didn't want to upset him all over again. I had to corner George and poke him with a stick until he told me more about Mom. Where was she? Had he talked to her again? Did he have her phone number?

But George didn't come home for dinner. He was probably driving around with Glenn and his buddies, smoking cigarettes, trying to find someone to buy them beer. I didn't tell Tom when he got home. I'd tell him after Teddy went to bed.

We ate dinner on trays in front of the TV. Dad didn't come downstairs. Right over our heads, he was stuck in his room—a black box filled with sadness. Last time, when Mom left, I'd tried going in there to get him up and he just rolled over and told me to get out. Not in a mean way but in an empty way, since the box he was in took all the life out of his voice. I'd known right off there was no point in yelling or begging or crying. He wasn't getting up.

44

At eight o'clock I sent Teddy to bed since he was falling asleep on the couch. When I went up to check on him I could hear Dad snoring through his door. He snored like some kind of diesel engine with a wet gurgle thrown in.

Teddy was in bed studying *Mike Mulligan and His Steam Shovel*. He couldn't read it yet, but he knew the words by heart since Mom used to read it to him all the time. She hated that book. "Got to go read about idiot Mike who dug himself into a hole. Story of my life. Rather stick pins in my eyes," she'd say on the way up the stairs.

I liked the story. It had a happy ending with Mike and his steam shovel, Mary Anne, set up in their cozy basement all safe and happy.

Teddy set the book down.

"Do you think they found Moocher yet?"

"Everyone's looking. I bet they have," I said. "Scootch over."

I lay down next to him and we shared his pillow while I read the story out loud. Teddy fell asleep halfway through and I read the rest to myself.

Back downstairs, Tom sat at the kitchen table while I did the dishes. Dad liked a neat kitchen when he made his coffee in the morning. I think he learned it from when he was in the army, where everything had to be what he called "spit polished." Yuck. If it wasn't clean he'd make a lot of grumpy noises while he wiped the crumbs off the counter or swept the floor.

I put the leftovers in the fridge hoping Dad might get up in the night hungry. He had two more days to sleep since Tuesday and Wednesday were his days off. Maybe that would be enough.

The Reds were playing the Cardinals. Tom and I sat on the couch and watched the game. When the commercials came on I poked Tom on the shoulder.

"George took the money."

Tom stared at me. "He said so?"

"Yeah. Mom called. Got him to do it."

"Mom called?"

He got real still and his face went splotchy red.

"A couple of months ago."

"Where is she?" He said it so softly I could barely hear him.

"Don't know. I guess she's got an apartment or something."

"She's not coming back, then."

I didn't answer. Tom turned away.

The game came on with lots of baseball talk about the pitcher's curveball, while the umpire swept the dirt off home plate. We watched, not talking. The batter struck out and threw his bat across foul territory. I understood how he felt.

"Are you gonna tell him?" Tom kept his eyes on the TV.

"Dad?"

He nodded.

"Not now. Not while he's up there."

We watched the game. Tom didn't ask any more questions. When things were rough he went silent or disappeared into the basement. And he kept busy with Carlos—doing their paper route, playing pickup baseball games, just running around. Tom tried to skim along on the surface of our screwed-up family like he was on a surfboard riding a dangerous wave.

But when Mom left he didn't always stay above water. Once, on a Saturday afternoon, I found him in Dad's room, under the covers, all alone, crying. He turned away and hid his face. "Taking a nap," he'd said. But we both knew he was lying. Teddy came in and all three of us got under the blanket, lay on our backs, and studied the cracks in the ceiling. "I see a hippo," Teddy said. Tom laughed a little. "That's a rhino, not a hippo," he said. "It's even got that big horn on its nose."

The score was tied, 2–2. I didn't really care who won.

It wasn't the same without Dad in his recliner, drinking a beer, insulting the batters or the umps. Even if there wasn't a baseball game on, Dad asleep in his chair, snoring, his big toe sticking out of a hole in his sock was way better than this quiet that filled the house with the TV blaring in the background.

Chapter 8

My alarm rang at five in the morning. I'd set it early enough so I could grab George before he went to work at the Far Reach. Tom and Carlos sat on the floor in the living room folding newspapers into tight rectangles for throwing onto porches and stoops. The truck delivered them in a tied-up stack at five every morning.

Teddy wasn't awake yet. George sat at the kitchen table eating a bowl of cereal.

"I need Mom's phone number," I said.

"In your dreams." He shoveled another spoonful of Cheerios into his mouth.

It had gotten real quiet in the living room. I knew the boys were listening, but Tom would stay out of it.

He was like one of those little moons orbiting Jupiter, keeping a safe distance.

"She's my mom, too," I said. "I've got to talk to her."

"If she wanted to talk to you she'd have called you already."

I couldn't believe he said that. I couldn't believe George could be so mean.

"You're a rotten brother."

He looked up. "You don't get it, do you? She couldn't take any of this anymore, especially Dad. It's his fault."

"His fault? What did he do?"

George ignored me, finished his cereal, got up, and put his bowl in the sink.

"Let it go, Nellie."

"If I let it go everything's gonna fall apart. I just want her number." I was begging. I hated to beg George for anything but I had no choice. "I have to talk to her. Dad's in bed, and when you left yesterday, Teddy melted into a crying, snotty mess. Please."

George looked at me straight on. He hadn't really looked at me in a long, long time. I didn't look away. He reached into his back pocket and pulled out his wallet. It was the wallet Dad got him for his birthday last year with a dollar in it, too, for good luck. George pulled a slip of paper out of one of the credit card slots.

I yanked the sea-green crayon out of Teddy's box of Crayolas.

George read out the number as I copied it down on a piece of paper towel.

He put the slip of paper back in his wallet.

"Thanks," I said.

He turned and banged out the back door.

I put Teddy's crayon in the box, stuffed the paper towel in the back pocket of my shorts, and went into the living room. The boys had loaded up their *Boston Herald American* shoulder bags with newspapers. Carlos patted Tom on the shoulder in the klutzy way boys do to be nice.

"You gonna call her?" asked Tom.

"Yeah," I said. It was hard to breathe and my stomach was cramped up.

I watched them from the front stoop as they zoomed down the street on their bikes in the new light, so free. I wanted more than anything to jump on my bike and peddle hard to catch up. But I'd gotten too tall—my knees knocked against the handlebars when I peddled.

The street was quiet and there was a breeze. I sat down on the stoop. Mom had taught me how to ride a bike. My red Schwinn with the pink tassels on the handgrips used to be Fiona's down the street. Back then the bike had been too big for me and I was scared to try. Mom made me do it. "Don't be chicken. Get on the damn thing already. I won't let go until you tell me to. Promise."

And Mom hadn't let go. She'd run behind me as I pedaled and wobbled and squeaked a little because I thought Mom might let go even though she promised she wouldn't. I kept pedaling and Mom kept running. "You got it! You got it!" she yelled, right there behind me, holding on to the edge of the seat, breathing hard, keeping up.

"I got it!" I yelled. "Let go!"

Mom let go and I pedaled hard, perfectly balanced, the pink streamers flying out around my arms.

My red Schwinn was in the basement now. I should give it to the Haberman twins. They could share it like they shared everything.

I sat there on the stoop. Leaned over and hugged my knees. I didn't want to think about any of it, didn't want to see one of the Haberman twins grinning, pedaling down the sidewalk on my bike. Mom had broken her promise after all. The one moms don't have to say out loud. She'd let go of me. And I didn't want to call her.

Chapter 9

Boston Herald American, July 16, 1974
3 Test-Tube Babies Born

I sat on the stoop until Tom and Carlos were long gone. When I went back in the house I kicked the door shut behind me like George did all the time. It helped a little. I opened the door and kicked it shut again.

Teddy, in his pj's, stopped halfway down the stairs and stared at me.

"I'm just mad," I said. His face crumpled up. "Not at you, silly."

"Okay," he said.

Tom had left Dad's newspaper on his chair. I picked it up and went into the kitchen. Teddy followed me and got busy coloring since the cartoons didn't start until six.

"Hey look!" I said, holding up the paper. "They found Moocher!"

Teddy smiled the biggest smile I'd seen in ages. He reached out and touched the photo of Moocher right there on the front page. "Read it to me," he said.

I read him the article all about the man in Natick the cops had arrested and the pet store owner who'd turned him in for trying to sell stolen birds. The parrot thief had hidden Moocher in his basement. The parrot was back now with Minnie and their chicks at the Stoneham Zoo.

"But why did he steal him?" asked Teddy when I finished reading the article.

"To sell him. For the money. Mean, huh?"

"Really mean. But Moocher's back."

"Yeah," I said. And I knew why Teddy's smile was gone now. "And Dad will be back soon, too, you'll see."

"Like last time."

"Exactly. He'll get tired of sleeping and go to work like always."

Teddy picked up his gray crayon and started coloring in a skyscraper. He'd used something like twenty colors to fill in the rainbow windows and they made me smile.

There was an article on the front page about the first three test-tube babies born in the history of the world. They put an egg in a test tube, added the sperm, shook it up or something, let it grow for a week, then put it inside the mother. How big was it after a week? And how did they get it back inside her? It was creepy.

We saw pictures of sperm in health class and they looked like tadpoles with skinny tails. Sperm. Ewww.

I turned to my horoscope. It was way off, as usual.

Taurus: You should be full of bright ideas now; ready, willing, and able to carry them out. Fine stellar influences stimulate ambitions and incentive.

Yeah, sure. Loads of *bright ideas* like calling Mom and getting Dad's money back.

Mom's horoscope made her out to be some kind of artist—*An excellent day for all creative activities.* Not likely. I knew for a fact that she couldn't even draw a decent stick figure.

I got two bowls from the cupboard. George had left the milk out as usual. When I set his bowl down next to him, Teddy shook his head and kept coloring. I ate my Cheerios while I read the comics. *Peanuts* was kind of dumb but *Hägar the Horrible* was funny. The thing about comics is the funny lasts for about two seconds and, *poof*, it's gone. The laugh or smile never lasts long enough to change much of anything.

Dad wasn't up. He always got up early, even on his days off. Tuesdays he'd drive to the Stop & Shop in Porter Square and get groceries. In the afternoon he'd take a nap in his recliner after he read the newspaper. Lately he'd been throwing the paper on the floor after reading about how Congress was going after President Nixon and all his aides. "It's a damned witch hunt!" he'd holler, and pull the lever to lower the back on his recliner. It would clunk into place, and he'd stretch his aching feet out and fall asleep for a good hour. He wouldn't wake up no matter what kind of racket we were making. "If a person can sleep in a war zone," he'd say, "he can sleep anywhere."

"Eat your cereal," I said to Teddy. "We've gotta go to the Far Reach."

"Why?"

"Just eat your cereal."

He didn't even look up from his coloring book, just shook his head again. The kid would starve to death if I didn't make him eat. I shoved his bowl of cereal toward him. Some milk slopped out and came close to soaking the picture he was working on.

"Hey!" he said. But he closed up his book and started eating.

Teddy finished his cereal and ran upstairs to get dressed while I washed the breakfast dishes. I didn't leave a note for Dad. We weren't going to be long and it's not like he'd notice we were missing.

Halfway down the block we ran into Mrs. O'Neill carrying a grocery bag up to her house. She always wanted to talk forever. I figured she was lonely because Fiona had moved away.

"Teddy, you're getting so big," she said.

He hid behind me. She loved to pinch him on the cheek so hard his eyes watered. He called her the crab lady with the pincers.

"Hi," I said.

"Hello, dear. I'm just getting back from the market," she said. "You two are up early."

"Yup." I scanned her weedy front yard. Teddy poked me in the back trying to get me moving. "Hey, I was wondering, do you have any garden work that needs doing? I'm trying to make some money."

"Let me talk to Mr. O'Neill."

"Great. I don't charge much."

"Come by later," she said, her purse slipping down her arm while she clutched the grocery bag. "Got to run, put the ice cream in the freezer."

"Need help?" I said. Teddy poked me again.

"Aren't you sweet? No, I'm fine."

Once she was in her house I laughed. "You lucked out, Teddy. Saved from the crab lady by melting ice cream." He nodded and ran ahead down the sidewalk.

When Mom left, most of the neighbor ladies had come by the house. They brought casseroles and offered to "help with the kids," whatever that meant. For weeks, one after the other, Mrs. O'Neill, Mrs. Mendez, Mrs. Moretti, all of them kept showing up at the front door. The first week, Dad was in bed and he either didn't hear the knocking or he was ignoring it like he ignored us. Tom and me took turns answering, lying about where Dad was, lying about how we were doing just fine. We ate the casseroles. The second week, when Dad was out of bed, he answered the door and turned away all those ladies. He wasn't exactly rude but they got the message and left us alone.

Teddy and me made it the rest of the way without running into anyone we knew. The Far Reach stood out from a mile away since it was shaped like a railroad car and was the only one-story building on the block. It was covered on the outside with shiny chrome and red panels that looked like glass.

When we got to the steps up to the door Teddy stopped.

"I'll wait out here."

I knew he was avoiding Fannie and her bone-crushing hugs. What was it with older ladies going around hugging and pinching little kids? They just couldn't help themselves.

"Fine," I said. "But stay put."

I pulled open the heavy glass door. The diner wasn't so shiny on the inside. Most of the booths had red, fake-leather seats, patched with matching duct tape. The long counter was worn out, with nicks and scars on top. But I liked the smell of the place—burgers, fries, meat loaf, roast chicken, onion rings—all mixed together.

Fannie was behind the counter holding a coffee pot. She had on her blue waitress dress with a white apron.

"Nellie!" she hollered. "What're you doing here?"

I waved and sat on one of the twirly stools at the counter.

"Be right back, darling," she called, and headed over to a back booth with the coffee.

Fannie loved everybody. Not in a phony way, but really and truly. All the regular customers, the old guys who sat on the stools at the counter and drank coffee, teased her and joked around and she gave it right back. But not with the paper-cut edge that Mom used when she joked. Dad said Fannie went to more funerals than anyone he knew. Whenever one of her customers died she'd be there in the church crying her eyes out.

She was short and solid, kind of busting out of her uniform in the back, and wore those shoes that laced up the sides that looked like rowboats. She was eggs sunny-side up—all smiles, even though her feet hurt, her husband, Tony, was dead, and her daughter, Patty, had moved to Florida with Fannie's "precious" grandbabies last year.

She came back behind the counter and stood opposite me, still holding the coffee pot. I fiddled with the ketchup bottle.

"What's up?" she asked.

"Not sure if Dad's gonna be here Thursday," I said in a low voice. I could see Lou, the owner, in the back at the grill.

"He in bed again?" Fannie turned and set the coffee pot on the machine.

"Yeah."

"What set him off?"

"It's complicated."

"Try me." She put her hands on her hips and waited.

I ignored her, which wasn't easy. But I didn't want to go into the whole story about George and my mom and the missing money. And I didn't want everyone in the diner to know my business. Fannie couldn't keep a secret to save her life.

The ketchup bottle was sticky. I set it down and rubbed my hand on my shorts.

"Can you cover for him if he doesn't show up on Thursday? Tell Lou he called in sick or something?"

"Sure, honey."

Fannie reached across the counter and stroked my cheek. It should have been no big deal but the feel of it got me close to tears. I pulled away.

"Gotta go," I mumbled.

"Nellie, you know you can talk to me, right? You got a lot on your plate right now."

"Yeah. Thanks, Fannie."

I twirled around on the stool and almost fell off trying to get out of there, trying to get away from her hand on my cheek that managed to unscrew the lid on the jar of all-alone sadness inside me. I was like one of those test-tube babies growing up in a glass tube in a laboratory with no parents around. But *they* only had to be in that tube for a week.

Outside the Far Reach I stood on the stairs and took a couple of deep breaths. Teddy sat on the bottom step trying to tie his sneaker. He was doing a lousy job.

I sat down on the stairs next to him, leaned over, and tied up his laces.

"I'm real glad Moocher's back with Minnie and the chicks," I said.

"Me too," he said.

I stood up, stuck my hand in my back pocket, and touched the paper towel where I'd written my mom's phone number in sea-green crayon. She wasn't a sunny-side-up kind of person like Fannie. She didn't stroke my cheek or tuck me into bed at night. But I might just die if she hung up on me.

Chapter 10

All morning Dad was up there in his bedroom. I called Maya but her mom said she was at St. Anthony's with her grandfather helping clean the rectory. Maya and him were buddies. She called him Vovo, which means *grandpa* in Portuguese, and he called her Querida, which means *sweetie*. Every summer they'd spend hours taking care of his grapevines, which filled up their whole entire backyard. He always let Maya and me help him pick the grapes in the fall. Her Vovo taught Maya how to spit, told her creepy ghost stories in Portuguese, and made homemade wine in their basement with his grapes.

I had other friends from school—Theresa, Lucy, Carmen. But only Maya understood about my mom gone and Dad in bed. If Maya was busy I'd rather hang out with Teddy, or Nancy Drew.

In the afternoon I started #8 while Teddy sat in his pool. Nancy Drew was eighteen and out of high school but she didn't have a real job. She zipped around in her blue convertible and never seemed to charge a dime for her detective work while she spent money right and left. She was a rich girl, which would make it easier to be brave and daring. If I was rich and didn't have to wash dishes or worry about bills piling up on the bookshelf in the living room, I'd be free to carry out loads of *bright ideas* like my horoscope said.

All day I put off calling Mom. The weight of Dad upstairs got heavier and heavier. The last time he'd done this I'd been in school during the day and only had to sit in the house at night while he was in his room, over my head, in the dark. But that first time, *Mom* being gone was brand new. Every day Dad was up there with the shades pulled down I'd expected her to come home and walk in the door, full of wisecracks as usual. Tom and me decided there was a chance she'd just taken a break, a vacation from dishes and laundry and us. But I knew even then, deep down, that she wouldn't have carted off her record player and all her records if she wasn't leaving for good.

The first couple of days after she left, the fridge was

packed with casseroles from the neighbors but we'd run out of milk and cereal and bread. I'd gone into Dad's room and he'd ignored me like a lump under the covers. His pants were on the floor in a heap. I pulled his wallet out of the back pocket and took ten bucks for groceries. Tom and Teddy and me walked to the Stop & Shop after school. That whole week was like living in one of those stories where orphans are left to fend for themselves in the woods or something.

At six o'clock I heated up a couple of cans of Spaghet-tiOs with meatballs—Teddy's favorite. Tom, Teddy, and me sat on the couch, ate our dinner, and watched a rerun of *Lost in Space* while the darkness in Dad's bedroom drifted down the stairs.

I sent Teddy up to bed at eight and Tom and me watched *Hawaii Five-O*. There was a chase scene in the end with helicopters and speedboats. It was hard to understand why there'd be any criminals for the cops to chase in a place with palm trees and beaches and warm weather all year round. During the ads I checked on Teddy. He was asleep with his book under his arm and the sheet kicked off his bed. I put the sheet up over him and went back downstairs.

Tom had turned the TV off.

"Did you call her?" he said.

"Not yet."

He didn't say anything.

"Listen," I said. "I'm gonna try to make some money for the Rushmore trip. Got any ideas?"

"I'll talk to Carlos."

"And I'll keep trying to squeeze some money out of George."

Tom laughed.

"Yeah," I said.

Upstairs, my room was too hot for a blanket but not hot enough for just a sheet so I stuck my feet out from under the covers to cool off. I hated having a room all to myself. Teddy and me had always shared a bedroom since he was born and he was six now, so that was close to half my life. But when I got my period for the first time in April on the class field trip to the Museum of Science, Dad had gotten spooked.

The day it happened I walked over to the Far Reach after I got home from school. I told Fannie and she gave me a big hug, drove me over to Walgreens, and got me a box of Kotex. But telling her was a big mistake. Fannie whispered the news into Dad's good ear, the left one, and he grabbed his toolbox that same night, dismantled

Teddy's bed frame and put it back together again in Tom and George's room. They couldn't hardly move in there now with the three beds, and there was only enough floor space for a two-person Monopoly game.

I missed Teddy at night. I was stuck with him all day but the nighttime was different. He'd almost always be asleep when I turned off my light and I liked the sound of him kicking the covers, which he did when he was dreaming. At least I was pretty sure he was dreaming. Not bad dreams since he didn't cry out or wake up scared. He dreamed a lot of hundred-yard-dash dreams.

Now with him gone there was a big empty space. The green carpet was fluffier and the color was brighter where his bed used to be. It was hard to fall asleep with no kicking noises, and the missing bed, a bed that I used to be able to almost touch when I reached across the gap.

I pulled the blanket off and rolled over. I'd gotten my period one more time and it hardly counted since it was over in two days. The whole thing was probably a false alarm. And on top of moving Teddy out, Dad started acting funny. His hugs got weird. Not that they happened all that often, but when he hugged me on my birthday in May, he was all stiff and faraway like a hug some adult gives a kid when they don't know them too well.

And Mom wasn't there that day when I came home from the Museum of Science with my sweatshirt tied around my waist to hide the big stain on my jeans. Mom wasn't around to tell Dad he was being a jerk when he carried his toolbox up from the basement. Without Mom there to crack jokes about my tiny boobs and two-day periods and make it halfway normal, Dad had gone and put me in solitary confinement like Steve McQueen in *The Great Escape* when the Nazis kept putting him in that tiny room alone, with his rubber ball that he threw against the wall over and over to keep from going nuts. I saw that movie with Maya on TV and it was the saddest movie ever.

If Mom hadn't left, I wouldn't feel like such a freak, being a girl. And Teddy'd be right there in his bed in our room kicking the covers off and drooling on his pillow. I was never going to fall asleep thinking about calling her and how she might hang up on me. And how I was the only girl in the house and it was me who had to fill that Maxwell House coffee can full of money so Dad would get out of bed and our whole family wouldn't go down the tubes.

Chapter 11

Boston Herald American, July 17, 1974
*Counsel Doar Will Urge Panel to
Recommend Impeachment*

It was a good thing Dad didn't get out of bed Wednesday morning. It said in the paper that the special counsel wanted Congress to impeach President Nixon for high crimes and misdemeanors. *High crimes* sounded really serious and *misdemeanors* sounded like no big deal but added together it was trouble.

For months last year, Dad and I watched the Watergate hearings on TV. "It's a lot of hot air," Dad said. Back then, what I liked most about the hearings was watching them with my dad. He'd call upstairs to get me. "Nell, it's on." And we watched together. Day after day.

A lot of people complained their regular shows got interrupted when the hearings came on. Mrs. O'Neill was furious when her soap operas got canceled. Mom hated all of it. When the president went on TV and told everyone, "I am not a crook," she laughed. Dad got real quiet. I wanted to tell her to shut up. She laughed even louder. "You're a fool, Ron. He *is* a crook. Just look at him." Dad got up, grabbed his wallet, stomped out the door, and headed to Benny's Tavern around the corner. They never had big fights. He always walked out the door first or went to bed.

What really ticked me off was that I was starting to think Mom was right. The more I'd learned from reading the papers and watching the news, it sure seemed like Nixon *was* a crook. His aides in the White House were all going to jail. Pretty fishy. But I'd never tell Dad. He was loyal and believed in his president with all his heart. To Dad, presidents were supposed to be almost like superheroes—strong, honest, fighting for the little guy, protecting the country. If Nixon turned out to be a crook, Dad's heart was gonna get broken again. I didn't see how he'd ever get over it.

I flipped through the newspaper to the horoscopes. Yesterday it said I'd have lots of success but now it sounded like maybe that wasn't so true.

> *Taurus: Review past failures, past successes. There's something to be learned from both. Incorporate the superior into any new effort. You can attain.*

Attain what? Big bucks? I wasn't sure if I'd ever had any great successes. Not like Nancy Drew, who'd saved lots of lives and rescued loads of people. On page one, book #1, she'd saved a little girl from drowning. Maybe by the time I was an old lady sitting on my porch I'd have more failures and successes to work with, but reviewing what I'd done so far wasn't much help.

Mom's horoscope recommended that she should *transform scintillating ideas into brisk quality actions. Scintillating* sounded like something shiny and wonderful. If she was sitting in her chair across from me, smoking her cigarette, she'd make some crack about the *scintillating* load of dirty laundry in a pile by the washing machine.

Maybe now that she was off on her own, reading her horoscope without that heap of greasy work clothes to deal with, she was coming up with loads of *scintillating ideas* and *quality actions.* Did she read my horoscope, too? Did she wonder what I was going to *attain* today? I folded the paper up since I didn't want to imagine what she was doing. And horoscopes were a bunch of baloney. She'd said so herself.

Teddy was watching *The Flintstones* and Fred's "Yabba dabba do!" was making him giggle like always. I put my cereal bowl in the sink and called Maya.

"Want to do the swans with us?" I said.

"Swans again?"

"We'll come over."

Tom was off somewhere with Carlos. I ran upstairs and got dressed. I picked up the Boston Red Sox mug off my bureau, dumped all the hopscotch stones out, and found my favorite—a black, smooth stone with a notch on one edge. I jammed it in my pocket.

In the kitchen I packed the stale bread from the Far Reach that Dad brought home once a week into the canvas bag Teddy called his bread bag. It was Mom's old school bag from when she was a kid, faded green with a loop that cinched it closed.

It was her fault Teddy was crazy about the swan boats and feeding the birds. Two or three times a week, when Mom got home from work and he got off the school bus, they'd go to the Boston Public Gardens. "Got to get out of this dump," she'd say. Dad would be in his recliner reading one of his history books and just shaking his head and mumbling, "Dirty dishes in the sink, supper to make, but you go ahead." "Bet your bottom dollar I will," she'd snap back. So Teddy got hooked on those boats and the birds and we'd been going all summer.

I called into the living room. "Wanna visit the swans?"

"Okay."

"Go get dressed."

Maya's apartment was over her family's store on

Highland Ave.—Manny's Convenience, six blocks away. Manny was her dad's name. He and Mrs. Machado were teenagers when they came to the US from the Azores, a bunch of islands in the Atlantic Ocean. Maya's never been there, but loads of people from the Azores lived in the neighborhood.

When we got there, Teddy pushed the door open and ran over to the shelf with the bacalao—dried, salted codfish, stacked up like wooden shingles. He picked one up with both hands—a big one, two feet long, with prickly fins and tail. I'd been to Sunday dinner at the Machado's a bunch of times, and Maya's mom made fish cakes from the bacalao they sold. They were way better than the fish sticks from the Far Reach.

Mrs. Machado came out from behind the counter. She was older than Mom. Her black hair was going gray and stuck to the back of her damp neck. She wore sandals and a dark-blue dress, with an apron that mostly covered her whole front and a gold cross around her neck.

"Mi querido!" she said to Teddy and laughed. "Maybe you'll be a fisherman when you grow up."

He smiled up at her and she leaned down and gave him a kiss on his forehead.

"Nellie," she said, holding her arms out. Fannie was a joker and Mrs. Machado was strict and no-nonsense but they both hugged. Mom was never big on hugs. If one of us kids fell down and was bleeding she'd get the Band-Aids out and clean up the blood, but that was it. No hugs. "Watch where you're going, for God's sake," she'd say.

Mrs. Machado was squeezing me like a lemon when Maya came through the back door that led upstairs to their apartment.

"Mama, let her go."

Mrs. Machado stepped back and eyed Teddy, who was walking down the aisle with the stiff codfish in his hands, swooping it up and down like it was swimming.

"Where you going with the fish?" said Maya.

He turned around and pointed it toward the shelf.

"What are you three up to?" asked Mrs. Machado.

"Taking Teddy to the playground and over to Nellie's house," Maya lied.

There was no way in a million years her mom would let her go on the subway without an adult. She couldn't even go to Porter Square alone. But Maya was an expert at sneaking around and it's not like we were smoking cigarettes or ducking into R-rated movies. Teddy was excellent camouflage.

"Be home by two," said Mrs. Machado in her no-fooling-around voice.

"Yes, Mama," said Maya.

Outside, Teddy walked ahead of us carrying his bread bag. We had to take a roundabout route, six blocks out of our way so none of Mrs. Machado's friends would spot us and report back.

"I got Mom's phone number out of George," I said.

Maya whistled. "You gonna call her?"

"I've got to get the money back."

"She's probably spent it already."

I didn't answer. We kept walking.

It was crowded on the subway. Teddy clutched the bread bag to his chest. I held on to his free hand, and Maya and I grabbed hold of the same pole by the middle door on the train. At Park Street Station we climbed the stairs and came out onto the Boston Commons filled with people moving slowly in the heat.

We joined the crowds crossing Charles Street into the Boston Public Gardens. Joey was at the crosswalk with his cart that was rigged up on the front of a bicycle. I rolled my eyes. He lived a couple of blocks from me on Truman Street and used to hang out with George. But after a fight at Nico's Pizza even George said Joey was trouble. His dad did a good business hustling overpriced cold sodas to hot tourists all summer. Joey got a prime location.

Maya waved.

"Hey," said Joey.

He was too cool for his own good.

I stood on the sidewalk and watched the two of them get all perky like they were on camera or something.

"Can I go?" said Teddy.

I nodded and he took off running down the path to our bench, the bread bag bouncing against his legs.

Maya smiled a flirty, phony smile and turned her back on Joey. Playing hard to get.

When we got to the bench Teddy was already standing in the grass by the lagoon crumbling stale hamburger buns around his feet. The first pigeon arrived—a pretty one with white racing stripes on her wings. She stood close to Teddy's feet and jabbed at a crumb with her beak. Soon there were a couple dozen pigeons surrounding him. He turned in a slow circle dropping crumbs and larger chunks on the ground.

Maya jabbed me with her elbow. "I finished number four."

"Which one's that?"

"*Mystery of Lilac Inn*."

"That's a good one. Scary."

"Yeah, especially when Nancy's out there in the woods at night. My mom would have a heart attack if I was running around like her."

"You've got the next one, right?"

"Already started it."

We were quiet, watching Teddy and his pigeons.

"What if my dad doesn't get out of bed this time?" I said.

"How long can he stay up there?"

"I don't know, but he could get fired. Then what? Money's already tight with just his paycheck."

"Your mom, she's . . ." Maya spit in the grass.

I smiled.

"Crook's here," Teddy called. He crouched down holding a chunk of bread for a scruffy pigeon with splashes of black and white and gray running down her body and a crooked beak where the top pointed part didn't meet the bottom.

"Hey, Crook," Teddy whispered.

"Ugly thing," said Maya under her breath.

"Yeah," I said. "But he loves her."

"Weird kid," she said.

"He's okay."

She stood up. "I'm gonna get a soda. Want one?"

"No, thanks."

She started back toward Charles Street and the vendors and their carts. From the way she was fussing with her hair, I knew Maya wasn't really thirsty. She just wanted to stand around and talk stupid with Joey.

Teddy walked down to the edge of the lagoon where the ducks were gathering. But he didn't start tossing bread right away. He stood there and studied the foot-bridge and the walkways, probably making sure he hadn't missed any pigeons.

Teddy didn't need fancy vacations or amusement parks to make his day. Just a bag of stale bread and a flock of birds. But I'd really been counting on our big road trip. Nancy Drew was always going on exotic trips to other countries and on tons of vacations to horseback ride, swim, or sail. She always got into scary situations but had a lot of fun. I'd never even stayed in a real hotel or flown in an airplane. Last year Carmen flew on a plane to New York City at Christmas to visit her grand-parents. She'd thrown up three times. She said they had little bags on the plane just for puking.

Dad always used to take all four of us to Fenway Park to see a home game in July or August. It was just a train ride away but it was a big deal for us. Mom never went. "Baseball's gotta be the most boring spectator sport ever invented," she'd said. We'd sit in the cheap seats way high up and Dad would buy us hot dogs and popcorn and sodas and he'd yell at the umpire. "You couldn't make the right call if you had a phone book!" "Take a nap *after* the game, Blue!" He'd laugh. We all laughed. And we cheered when the Sox got a hit, even Teddy, who didn't have a clue what was going on. "The Red Sox are our team, kids, win or lose," Dad would say as we trooped out of the ballpark with the crowds, Teddy sitting up on his shoulders so he didn't get lost.

There weren't gonna be any trips to Fenway this summer.

A couple of Teddy's ducks were quacking now, squabbling over a chunk of hot dog bun floating in the water. He pulled a big handful of bread out of the bag as more ducks swam over in twos and threes. He always tried to make it fair—scattering bread as far as he could for the shy ones, swinging his throwing arm wide like Lawrence Welk, the conductor on TV, waving his baton.

I leaned down and picked up a handful of gravel from under the bench and threw it at a tree trunk. The little pings the rocks made weren't very satisfying. I wiped my hands off on my shorts and kicked the gravel under the seat again. Why couldn't Maya just stick to whistling and spitting?

Chapter 12

Maya had ditched me and I was stuck there on that park bench scratching a hole in the dirt with my sneaker. One of the swan boats floated by with only half its seats filled. Teddy watched from the water's edge. A teenage boy sat on the tractor seat inside the giant white swan in the back of the boat pedaling like crazy. I could walk faster than those boats, and the lagoon was pretty sad as far as ponds or lakes go—small and so shallow I could make out all the beer cans and trash sitting on the bottom.

Teddy stood very still, his empty bread bag on the ground, watching as another swan boat floated by filled with a Girl Scout troop, each of the girls wearing their green uniforms with sashes covered with merit badges.

When Maya and I were in second grade we decided after one meeting of the Brownie troop at Saint Norbert's Catholic Church that it was too much like school. We figured we'd rather ride our bikes or play hopscotch than have some Brownie lady tell us what to do with our free time.

The swan boat slipped under the footbridge and Teddy came over and sat next to me, holding his cap and the bread bag on his lap. I scrubbed his head. His crew cut was all stubbly. He smiled up at me.

"Let's go find Maya," I said.

We found her drinking a soda, leaning up real close to Joey next to his cart.

"We're heading home," I said, trying to put as much ice in my voice as I could on such a hot day. "You coming?"

Maya ignored the ice and smiled. "I'm gonna hang around here for a while."

I didn't say anything. I wanted to tell her she was just as big a jerk as Joey. But I didn't. Grabbing Teddy's hand, I started across the street.

I stuffed my other hand in my pocket and pulled out my hopscotch stone. I wanted to pitch it across the street right at Maya's head. I never knew anymore who was gonna turn up—the regular Maya who I'd known forever or the Maya who'd been taken over by aliens and had just dumped me for a boy.

Like always, there was a big group of hippies sitting on the grass in the Commons. They stood out with their tie-dye clothes, bell-bottomed jeans, long hair, and twirly skirts. One of them was playing the guitar. It was Wednesday afternoon and none of them were at work, and they were sure old enough to have jobs. Dad said they were bums, living off their rich parents. But I liked the look of them—all the color and smiles and singing.

On the train Teddy knelt on the orange plastic seat with his face planted on the glass window looking for rats. In the tunnel it was pitch-black out the windows, except for the red flashes of emergency lights. Tom said he and Carlos once saw a string of big Norway rats running along a ledge between Central Square and Porter Square.

The subway calmed me down after wanting to give alien Maya a swift kick or maybe just cry. The *clink* and *clank* moving through the tunnel under the city, the flashes of pipes and cables and thick dirt on the walls kept my attention. The train windows flicked on and off in the blackness, becoming mirrors so I could study the faces of the passengers in the glass without them knowing.

A tall kid, really tall, with an Afro that made him taller, sat next to Teddy. I studied his reflection in the window across from us. He had a kitten hidden in his jacket, sticking its head out under his chin.

Teddy reached over and petted the kitten's head. The kid smiled down at him.

"What's his name?" asked Teddy.

"Champ," said the boy.

"Hi, Champ."

"Gotta hide him now," said the boy, pushing the kitten deeper inside his jacket. "They don't let pets ride the train."

"Okay," said Teddy, and he turned back to his search out our window.

When the train climbed out of the tunnel Teddy and I blinked in the bright summer light.

"No rats," he said.

The train clattered across the Salt and Pepper Bridge over the Charles River and rushed underground again.

When we climbed the stairs to the street at Porter Square we both slowed down. At the playground I stopped. The hopscotch court was right there next to the fence. I hadn't called Mom and I didn't want to go home with Dad stuck in his bedroom.

"I'm gonna play a quick game," I said to Teddy.

"Okay," he said.

That's when the barking started. It was coming from

a few blocks away. Not ferocious or anything, more like a sad howl. Over and over. A "help me" bark. I knew I should have ignored it, headed straight to the hopscotch court and pitched my stone onto the first square. But I didn't.

Chapter 13

The dog was tied up with a rope on the porch of a green house. A big man in a blue bathrobe was hitting him. He whacked the dog with a sneaker over and over. He hit the dog on his nose and on his back. The rope got tangled around the man's ankles as the dog tried to crawl under the beat-up couch on the porch.

"Hey!" I yelled. "You're hurting him!"

The man turned and stared at me. His lips curled up all ugly-mean. He looked like he might jump down off that porch and hit *us* with the sneaker. Teddy grabbed my hand.

"Mind your own damn business, kid," the man said.

"You shouldn't hit him like that." I squeezed Teddy's

hand hard to keep myself brave. The dog lay flat on the wooden floor, whimpering. He was tied up. He couldn't escape. And even I knew a dog's nose was real sensitive.

"You want him?" the man said. "I'm done with him."

The dog inched away from the man's feet. He was scruffy with droopy ears and patchy brown hair. The rope pulled tight, tied to his collar in a rough knot.

"Really?"

"Steals food off the counter, won't sit, won't come."

Teddy jerked on my arm, stared up at me, and nodded his head, his eyes full of hope. A dog!

I swallowed. There was no way I could bring a dog home.

"Sure," I said. "We'll take him."

The guy untied the rope from the porch railing, dragged the dog down the steps, and handed me the frayed end.

"Don't think you can bring him back," he said.

I nodded.

He climbed up on the porch. "Now get lost." The screen door slammed behind him.

Teddy was already on his knees giving the dog a hug. Now I'd really done it. When we'd begged for a pet, Dad went on and on about dogs and cats and all the food they ate and the vet bills. "Get a goldfish," he'd said.

A dog wasn't gonna be easy to hide. They barked.

"Abe," said Teddy. "Dad says all we need is an Abe and we'd be a-okay."

"Yeah, fine." I hung on to the rope with both hands as the crazy dog tried to pull me into traffic. "Just tell Abe to sit."

"Abe, boy, come here." Teddy sat down on the sidewalk and the dog trotted over and licked his ear. Teddy giggled and gently shoved him away.

When we got to our block the Haberman twins were on the sidewalk in front of their house with identical pink jump ropes. They ran up to Abe, side by side, in their identical striped shorts and tops.

"He's so cute," said Maggie or maybe Jenn.

"Where'd you get him, Teddy?" asked Jenn or maybe Maggie.

"We rescued him."

Mr. Moretti sat on his porch smoking a stinky cigar. His poodle, Jack, barked extra loud when we got close. Abe wagged his tail. Mr. Moretti nodded and Teddy waved, grinning.

I had rope burns on my hands by the time we got home. Once we were inside the front yard I handed Abe over to Teddy. The latch on the gate was busted and Dad had used a bungee cord to hold it open. I shut it tight and wrapped the cord around the post.

"Let him go," I said.

Teddy struggled with the knot. I helped him get it loose while Abe sat there panting, spit dripping off the end of his tongue. I pulled the rope free and Abe went straight for the one bush in our yard and peed on it. He circled around the fence sniffing the ground, came back to Teddy, and sat in front of him waiting.

"What do you think he wants?" Teddy said.

"Probably water. Let's bring him inside."

Abe lapped up a bowl of water while we sat at the kitchen table and watched.

"How're we gonna hide a dog from Dad?" I said.

"Under your bed?"

"He's not gonna stay put."

"We'll get him really tired with walks," said Teddy, stroking Abe's back. "And we need dog food."

"Yeah, and a real leash." I rubbed at the rope burns. They sold dog food at Manny's Convenience but I didn't want to run into Maya after she'd deserted me at the swan boats. "They'll have leashes at the hardware store and we can get dog food at the Stop & Shop."

I went upstairs to my room and opened the closet door. The seventy-eight dollars I'd saved for my stereo was in a sock I'd hidden in the pocket of my winter coat. I was supposed to be adding to it to get us out West, not taking money out. But the dog had to eat. I counted out ten dollars and stuffed it in my front pocket.

If I could get the money back from Mom it wouldn't matter if I bought a lousy bag of dog kibble. In a couple of weeks Abe might be sitting in the back seat of Dad's Dodge Dart, his head stuck out the window, ears flying, as we drove west toward South Dakota.

"Won't happen if you don't call her," I whispered. "You're such a chicken."

Downstairs I found a pair of Dad's work gloves in the hall closet to protect my hands. We tied the rope back onto Abe's collar and headed to Porter Square. He wasn't such a bad dog. By the time we were half-way there he wasn't pulling much at all. And he wasn't a fighter, either. We ran into a woman walking a big German shepherd, twice the size of Abe. Both dogs were polite, just sniffed each other's butts.

"Why do they do that?" asked Teddy.

"They're saying hello," said the lady.

"Weird, huh?" I said. Teddy giggled.

At the hardware store in Porter Square, I left Teddy outside with Abe and went in and bought a leash with a soft loop at the end to hang on to. We untied the rope and clipped the leash onto his collar. Abe wagged his tail.

"Stay out here with him while I get the food," I said. "Put your hand through the loop so he doesn't get away."

The air-conditioning in the Stop & Shop was on full blast. I shivered. In the pet food aisle I picked out a ten-pound bag of the cheapest kibble and a box of dog biscuits. I also grabbed a three-pack of rawhide bones. He might stay quiet if he had one of those to chew on. Dad was right. Pets were expensive. I'd spent almost six dollars right off the bat.

Teddy held on to Abe on the trip back. That dog stopped to sniff every telephone pole, tree trunk, parking meter, and fire hydrant between Porter Square and our house.

"Why does he smell everything like that?" asked Teddy.

"Curious, I guess. Probably smells dog pee from years back."

"I think he sees with his nose," said Teddy. "A smell picture. In sixty-four colors."

I laughed even though I was sweating and my arms ached from carrying the grocery bag.

Back home Teddy filled a cereal bowl with kibble. Abe went crazy running in circles in the kitchen, his tail wagging, but he didn't bark, which was a good thing since Dad was right upstairs. Before Teddy even set the bowl down Abe stuck his nose in it and kibbles flew across the floor.

Tom and Carlos came in the back door while Abe was still eating and he didn't even look up. Not much of a guard dog.

"Where'd he come from?" asked Tom.

"We saved him from getting hit with a sneaker," said Teddy.

"Dad's gonna blow a gasket."

"We're gonna hide him."

Carlos laughed. "How're you gonna do that?"

"Under Nell's bed."

They both laughed. Abe finished his kibble and went up to each of them for a head scratch.

"Friendly," said Tom.

"Kinda ugly," said Carlos. "But doesn't bite."

They all got glasses of Kool-Aid and a handful of Oreos each and settled in the living room in front of the TV. Abe jumped on the couch and curled up next to Teddy.

I hid the bag of kibble in the hall closet, and picked up the water and food bowls and washed them in the sink. It was too bad Abe wasn't some little dog I could fit in a box or something. He must've known I was thinking about him because he jumped off the couch and came over to me for a scratch behind the ears.

"You kind of stink, you know," I said.

Abe wagged his tail.

Our dog, Dad's missing president, was the happiest creature in our house. It was funny in a sick kind of way considering how Abe Lincoln was assassinated.

Chapter 14

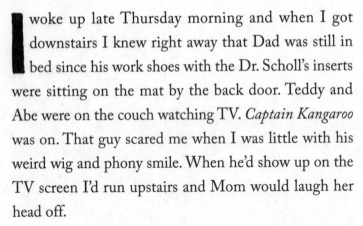

I woke up late Thursday morning and when I got downstairs I knew right away that Dad was still in bed since his work shoes with the Dr. Scholl's inserts were sitting on the mat by the back door. Teddy and Abe were on the couch watching TV. *Captain Kangaroo* was on. That guy scared me when I was little with his weird wig and phony smile. When he'd show up on the TV screen I'd run upstairs and Mom would laugh her head off.

Tom was back from his paper route, sitting at the kitchen table finishing his cereal. I knew he'd seen Dad's work shoes, too, but he didn't bring it up. Neither did I.

"We fed Abe," he said. "Sure does suck down the food."

"Kibble's not gonna last very long," I said.

"Carlos and me are gonna help people load their groceries in their cars at the Stop & Shop later. He said we can get tips. You know, for the Rushmore trip."

"Great!"

After a long stretch of quiet he said, "Did you call her?"

"Not yet."

He didn't say anything, just got up, opened the basement door, and disappeared. But I caught the look on his face right before he turned away. His eyes were shiny and squinched almost shut, like he had a stomachache. A bad stomachache. The kind our fourth-grade teacher, Mrs. Howard, had when she went home early and it turned out her appendix was ready to explode. But I didn't think Tom had anything wrong with his guts. I think he missed Mom, who should have been standing there at the sink complaining about the dog we dragged home. And he missed Dad, who should have been at work flipping burgers and dropping fries into the hot grease.

I sat down at the kitchen table. Captain Kangaroo was telling some story about a mouse wanting a house. I wished Teddy would shut the TV off. I wished I could put Joni Mitchell's *Blue* album on the record player and listen to her words as she sang her sad songs and not think about anything else.

I unfolded Dad's newspaper that Tom had left for him on the table. There wasn't any news about President Nixon on the front page for a change. But there was an article about a black storeowner, James Wilds, who got shot by the police. The protesters said, "Black life is cheap in Boston." The police didn't want any outside investigation, which proved the protesters right, didn't it?

There were hardly any black people living in our neighborhood. Dad said it was because of all the racists in Somerville and that Boston was way worse. He'd said, "I used to be a lot like the bigots in Southie but in the army, over in Korea, I learned pretty fast that the black guys had my back just like I had theirs."

James Wilds had a wife and three kids. Would his wife have to stand right where he'd been murdered while she stocked the shelves with peanut butter and ketchup? Mrs. Machado would cry forever if it had been her husband, Manny.

Reading the newspaper always got me stirred up because the news was almost always rotten. I should be like Maya and try to ignore all of it. Even Nancy Drew never seemed to be interested in politics or the news, just mysteries that turned up everywhere she went.

But even if I didn't make it to any more states this summer I was going to someday. I might have to take a Greyhound bus to do it since I didn't have a blue convertible like Nancy Drew, but I was gonna see it all. So it would probably help to know something about the world. And maybe, after that, I'd try to help fix it like Susan B. Anthony did.

I flipped to the comics since I needed a break from thinking about the real world. *Hägar the Horrible* was funny. Well, kind of funny.

My horoscope's advice was a day late. Abe was already sitting on the couch with Teddy.

> *Taurus: Hold off on making decisions and commitments until you are sure you have all the facts and do take into consideration the various dispositions and temperaments of those involved in your activities.*

I knew when I grabbed hold of the frayed end of that rope that Dad didn't have the right *dispositions* or *temperaments* to have a dog in the house. He was going to hit the roof when he found out. But sometimes there's just no other choice. We couldn't just walk away from that dog getting smacked on the nose.

Mom's horoscope said she should *think twice about all decisions related to travel and large purchases.* Where was she going and what was she spending the Mt. Rushmore money on? I could picture her in a cozy apartment, with Joni Mitchell on the record player, smoking a cigarette, reading her horoscope. Was she laughing? Or did she only make fun of it when I was around?

I got Teddy a bowl of cereal, brought it to him in the living room, and sat next to him and Abe. There was something about our dog that calmed the whole house down. He was just lying there, not doing much, but every time he caught me looking at him he'd slap his tail against the cushion. Happy. He was happy.

I looked over at Dad's recliner and his bookshelf along the wall. He'd read every one of those histories and biographies about Mt. Rushmore and the lives of those presidents he loved. He'd collected the camping gear we'd need and taped a map of the United States on the wall over the bookshelf with the route traced in red marker. All his planning had made him happy. And now his big trip was gone.

None of Dad's plans worked out so great. He'd gotten three out of four of the boys he wanted. Then Mom left. Just up and left. No note. No forwarding address. She just packed her powder-blue Samsonite suitcase, her record player, and her whole entire record collection and walked out on us. Connie Sanders up and disappeared on Friday, February 22, 1974. It was George Washington's birthday and I don't think that was an accident.

Now it didn't look like there'd be a baby Abe. Which made it even tougher for Dad. He'd lost Mom but if I'd turned up a boy thirteen years ago at least he'd have his four presidents all sitting around the TV watching *The*

Wonderful World of Disney in their pj's, making his heart beat extra fast with the happiness of a complete set. I didn't think Abe, the dog, was going to make it okay.

And we weren't ever the kind of family to be hanging out in our pj's together watching sappy TV shows. Tom spent half his life in the basement gluing his models together and George was always off with his caveman buddies driving around in Glenn's Chevy.

I wanted to call Maya but I was still mad at her for ditching me for Joey and that would get all tangled up with wanting to talk to her about calling my mom. So I curled up at the end of the couch with Abe's head resting on my legs and tried to ignore the weirdo Captain Kangaroo.

The commercials came on. I couldn't sit still. The weight of Dad upstairs might bring the whole house down soon. The second floor would drop and the building would flatten out like a pancake. Plaster and dust, scraps of furniture and torn books, cracked dishes and bent saucepans would fly up into the air and settle in a heap.

"Get dressed, Teddy. We're going out," I said.

He and Abe looked up at me.

"Where?"

"Yard work, I hope. At the O'Neills'."

He made a face, probably because Mrs. O'Neill was the crab lady with the pincers.

"Okay, stay here. But you and Abe have to hide in the basement with Tom. Dad might come down to eat something. Bring your coloring book with you."

"Okay."

I went upstairs to get dressed. Dad was in the hall, just leaving the bathroom, his back to me.

"Hi," I said, hardly breathing.

He lifted his hand in a tiny wave and kept walking toward his room. His hair on the back of his head was smashed down and his T-shirt was wrinkled up.

"I need money for milk," I said.

He disappeared into his room. I waited. He came back out and handed me a ten-dollar bill. He kept his eyes down. I took the money. It was worse seeing him. Worse than imagining him under the covers, half asleep.

When he got to his bedroom door he mumbled, "Sorry, Nell."

I stood there in the hallway as he closed the door behind him. I heard the creak of his old bed as he crawled back in. I'd wanted a "sorry" from Dad. I'd thought it would make it better. But it didn't, even though it sounded like a real sorry. If he was sorry why didn't he just take a shower, get dressed, and drive to the store and buy groceries himself? His "sorry" made it sound like he didn't have any choice. Like someone was in his room holding him hostage at gunpoint—a bank robber standing guard, with the tellers and the secretaries and the bank manager all huddled on the floor while the cops surrounded the building.

"We need the weeds pulled," said Mrs. O'Neill. "The yard raked and the bushes trimmed back off the fence."

Mr. O'Neill sat in a lawn chair and supervised. "Hold the edger with both hands." "Use your shoulders when you rake." "NO! That's not a weed." After two hours their yard was neat and tidy and I'd made two bucks. They should have paid me more with all the bossing around I had to put up with. I understood a lot better now why their grown-up daughter, Fiona, had moved to Melrose. But the good thing was I didn't think about the news or Dad or Mom since I was trying so hard not to bop the king of nags, Mr. O'Neill, over the head with the rake.

When I got back home Teddy was back to watching TV with Abe, and Maya was sitting at the kitchen table pouring herself a bowl of cereal.

"When did you get here?" I said.

"Just now. And you didn't tell me you got a dog!"

It was regular Maya, wearing flip-flops and no makeup. I stopped being mad before she even poured the milk on her Cheerios.

"Dad doesn't know about him yet," I said.

"Jeez, Nell. Are you nuts?"

"Kinda." I poured myself a bowl of cereal. "And I'm gonna call her today."

Maya looked over at me. Thinking. That's one of the things I liked about her. She wasn't the panicky type, never rushed into anything. But she wasn't a scaredy cat, either.

"When?"

"When we're done eating."

Maya scooped up a spoonful of cereal. Once a person poured milk on a bowl of Cheerios it was always a race—a race to finish before they got soggy with milk. We kept at it. Maya finished first.

"I can't believe your mom's been sitting in her own apartment this whole time."

I chased after the last few Cheerios floating around in my bowl with my spoon. Maya put our dishes in the sink and I put what was left of the milk in the fridge.

"Hey, Teddy," I called.

No answer. I got up and checked the living room. He and Abe were sitting on the floor two feet from the *Brady Bunch* on the TV screen. Good. I didn't want him to hear this phone call.

The paper towel with Mom's phone number on it was still in my back pocket. I pulled it out and smoothed it flat on the table.

"Now?" said Maya.

I nodded and pulled the phone off the receiver on the kitchen wall next to the fridge.

Maya whistled. It made me feel a little braver. I dialed the number. It rang forever. I twisted the phone cord up in my free hand. My stomach wasn't too happy with the Cheerios.

"Hello." It was my mom's voice.

"Mom?" There was a long, long pause. "Don't hang up."

"George called me. Told me he gave you my number. He shouldn't have."

That's all she had to say to me? Not, "Hi, honey," or "I miss you."

"Mom."

"Nellie, I know it's been hard on you. My leaving."

Her voice wasn't mean. But it wasn't a let's-have-a-chat voice, either. I looked up at Maya. I didn't say anything.

"Nellie? What do you want?"

What did I want? I wanted her to come home. I wanted her to say she felt awful for deserting me and everyone else in this house. I wanted to tell her I got my period on the school field trip to the Museum of Science and she was supposed to be there when I got home but she wasn't.

"You left. Maya and me went to Woolworths look-ing for you. They said you'd quit your job, too. And you didn't say goodbye. I thought you might be dead."

"Well, I'm not dead, am I?"

I wanted to tell her to go to hell. To slam the phone back on the receiver. I looked over at Maya again. She was nodding. Go for it. Ask.

"I want the money back. The five hundred dollars you stole from Dad."

"I don't have it. I needed rent money."

"You spent all of it?"

"Nellie, I think it's better we hang up now. You'll be fine with your dad."

"Dad's not fine. He's in bed. We have to get to Mt. Rushmore."

The phone clicked.

"She hung up on me!" I yelled.

"Call her back," said Maya.

I dialed the number again. I let it ring and ring and ring. My stomach flipped around and I gagged. The Cheerios. I dropped the phone and ran up the stairs and into the bathroom. I leaned over the toilet and threw up everything—sour orange juice from earlier and the Cheerios—and I kept on heaving once my stomach was empty. Maya got to the door.

"Jeez, Nellie. You okay?"

Between the dry heaves and tears running down my face I started laughing. Because it was kind of obvious I wasn't okay. And because I hated Mom right then. A crazy, red-hot hate.

I stood up, flushed the toilet, and rinsed my mouth out at the sink. My legs were wobbly. I sunk down on the bathroom floor and leaned against the edge of the tub. That's when I started sobbing. Big gulping sobs. Maya ran a washcloth under the tap and handed it to me. I wiped the puke and tears off my face and kept crying because Dad hadn't come running out of his room to rescue me from the hurt. He'd slept through it all. Weren't parents supposed to have built-in radar that screeched in their heads when their kids needed them?

Abe trotted into the bathroom, climbed in my lap, and licked my face. I cried even harder because a dog I hardly knew came to my rescue and my dad didn't.

Maya sat down next to Abe and me and put her arm around my shoulders.

I heard someone on the stairs. Tom appeared in the doorway.

"What's wrong?" he said.

"I called her." I wiped at my face with the washcloth. "Didn't go too good."

"Was she mean?"

"Yeah."

"Why're you in the bathroom?"

"She puked her guts out," said Maya.

"I hate her," I said.

Tom nodded.

I got up off the floor and grabbed Maya's hand to pull her up. I didn't really hate Mom enough. Because I still wanted her to come home. And the wanting her to come home hurt so bad. I didn't think she knew how badly she'd hurt me or she *would* come home. She'd have to.

Chapter 15

Maya and Tom and me walked single file down the stairs. Abe ran down ahead of us. Teddy was lying on the floor in the living room with his coloring book.

"I'm gonna find Carlos," said Tom, grabbing his baseball glove off the shelf by the back door. "We're going over to the Stop & Shop after the game."

"You okay?" I said.

He punched the pocket of his glove. Punched it hard. "Just wish this would all stop."

"Me too," I said.

Maya and me sat at the kitchen table. My stomach had settled down some but I wasn't ready to try eating another bowl of Cheerios.

"I've got seventy-two dollars plus the two I made today at the O'Neills'," I said.

"That money was for your stereo."

"Yeah, well, I guess Mom stole the music a second time when she swiped the five hundred bucks."

"God, Nellie. I thought my mom was bad. She won't hardly let me out of her sight. Yours is the worst."

She was the worst. She'd stolen way more than Mt. Rushmore. And I was going to even things out.

"I'm gonna have a yard sale," I said.

"What?"

"I'm gonna sell her stuff."

Maya leaned in closer across the table. "Your mom's stuff?"

I swallowed. My throat hurt.

"Yeah," I said. "All of it."

"Jeez, Nell."

"Saturday morning. Can you help?"

"Yeah, okay. We need to make signs and I'll bring my mom's cashbox and stickers. She's the queen of yard sales."

"We can't put up signs till Dad's at work on Saturday. He can't know about any of it. He'd flip his lid if he found out."

Maya got quiet.

"What?" I said.

"What if he doesn't go to work on Saturday?"

"Then it's off."

I couldn't think about Dad upstairs in bed or my stupid horoscope that said to *hold off on making decisions*. I got up and dug around in the bottom drawer in the kitchen cupboard by the sink and found construction paper and markers Mom kept around for our last-minute school projects. If we made the signs, the yard sale would have to happen. If we made the signs, Dad would have to get himself to work.

"Let's do it," I said.

YARD SALE!!!
WOMEN'S CLOTHES, JEWELRY, BOOKS
EVERYTHING MUST GO!!
234 CARLISLE STREET
9 A.M. TO NOON

It was good to be doing something. It was good to have Maya right there at the table with me. We finished ten signs and piled them up.

"I'm starving," I said.

"And I gotta get home. Mom gave me until two."

"Come early Saturday," I said.

I sat on the couch eating toast and reading #8 while Teddy colored in a picture of Batman's cave. I had a

107

headache from puking and couldn't concentrate on Nancy even though she'd been knocked out cold by the bad guy at the end of the last chapter and was tied up in an attic and I wanted to find out what was going to happen.

I'd hidden the signs for the yard sale in the hall closet with the dog food. There was a lot to sell. Dad had gotten a pile of empty boxes at the liquor store and packed it all up a couple of weeks after Mom left. Tom and Teddy and me watched as he went through the house packing her stuff—her sewing box on the shelf in the living room, her winter hats and coat and boots, her umbrella with seashell decorations she'd bought when we went to Nantasket Beach for fried clams.

I'd held on to Teddy's hand and stood close to Tom while we watched Dad, his face all tight and silent. Mom's stuff disappearing into those liquor boxes had made it real. No one could pretend anymore that she was coming back. And it didn't seem like Dad wanted her back. He'd made a racket slamming the closet door and banging drawers shut while he cleared their bedroom out—packed up all her clothes and makeup and her jewelry box that played a song when it got opened.

He wrote CONNIE in big black letters on the side of each box and stacked them on the shelves in the basement. He'd erased Mom from the house—it was full of holes when he was done, like Swiss cheese. The worst was their bedroom. There was no "Mom and Dad's room" anymore. I hated going in there now without her makeup on the bureau and her bathrobe on the back of the door.

I didn't want to open all those boxes on Saturday. It was going to be like picking off a scab. And what if she came back? It was kind of like stealing if I sold all her stuff. It was stealing.

"Teddy, get dressed," I said.

I had laundry to do, we needed milk, and Teddy was still in his pj's at three o'clock in the afternoon. I was the orphan who had to take care of the rest of the orphans. That's not how it worked in fairy tales. Snow White had the seven dwarfs to look out for her.

Once Teddy was dressed I got him to help me collect all the dirty laundry in the boys' room and my room and we piled it up in the kitchen. I wasn't too keen on doing George's laundry but Teddy had mixed it all up in the pile. I got the first load going in the washing machine and we left for Porter Square with Abe on his leash. There weren't many people walking around—too hot. It would be a perfect day to go to the movies, eat popcorn, and drink a cold soda, but I had to save my money.

Teddy stayed outside with Abe. I took my time in the Stop & Shop with the air-conditioning on full blast, enjoying a mini vacation from the heat wave outside. I only had the ten bucks Dad had given me so I stuck to the basics: milk, OJ, bread, hot dogs, bologna, cereal, and Oreos. I pocketed the change: fifty-seven cents.

By suppertime I'd washed, dried, and folded three loads of laundry. I took a long shower, washed my hair, and brushed my teeth again since my mouth still tasted sour from throwing up.

I was in the kitchen making franks and beans for dinner when Tom got home. He pulled a pile of change out of both front pockets of his shorts and dumped it on the kitchen table.

"Carlos gave us most of his tips," he said. "We must have loaded a hundred grocery bags into people's cars."

"Wow!" I said.

"We're going back tomorrow."

"Great. And I made a couple of bucks today doing yard work."

We watched *I Love Lucy* while we ate off trays in the living room. We even laughed a little when Lucy pretended to be a dancer on stage and spun around so hard she tipped the other dancers over. If Dad was sitting there we'd be watching the six o'clock news with Walter Cronkite while we ate dinner. Mom would be eating in the kitchen by herself, reading one of her mysteries. "Nixon gives me indigestion," she'd say.

* * *

George came banging into the house around eight.

"Where'd the dog come from? Saw him in Teddy's bed this morning when I got up."

"His name's Abe," said Teddy.

"So Dad's fourth president's a dog? That's about right," said George, laughing.

Abe jumped off the couch and walked up to him, tail wagging. George leaned down and gave him a pat on his head. That dog had a way with people—softened them right up.

"We're hiding him," said Teddy.

George looked at me. "Dad doesn't know?"

"Not yet," I said.

"Well, pooch," he said, patting him on the back. "Don't get too comfortable here."

He turned and went back in the kitchen. I heard him heating up some dinner. Before Mom left, if George was around he'd always eat with her in the kitchen while the rest of us watched the news. They'd talk in quiet voices while they ate. She'd laugh sometimes. When I brought my dishes in, the two of them sitting there looked so comfortable together. Now he was eating alone.

Even though I wanted to punch his lights out for taking the money, his aloneness made me want to go in there, sit with him, be another person in the room with

111

him. But George was so prickly he'd probably tell me to get lost.

After Teddy took Abe out to pee I sent them up to bed.

George went up, too, since he'd been awake since five in the morning for work. I cleaned the kitchen, and Tom and me stayed up late watching TV. Halfway through *The Streets of San Francisco*, right in the middle of a shoot-out, the yelling started.

"What the hell?" It was Dad.

Teddy came racing downstairs in his pj's with Abe right behind him. They both jumped up on the couch with Tom and me. Teddy pulled the afghan over Abe.

Dad stomped downstairs and stood in front of us. He was in his pajama bottoms and a white T-shirt. His hair was mussed up and his face was all creased from being smashed against his pillow for days. He glared at us.

"Where is it?"

"He's a secret," Teddy whispered.

"What?" Dad yelled.

Teddy jammed himself against the cushions like he was trying to get swallowed up. Tom turned and eyed me. George stood on the landing. He had a grin on his face. An I-told-you-so grin.

"It's a dog," I said.

"I know it's a dog," said Dad. "Where'd it come from?"

Abe crawled out from under the afghan, looked up at Dad, and wagged his tail.

"Damn it," he said. "I want it outta here. Now."

"The guy was hitting him. He was tied up," I said.

"I want that ugly mutt gone."

"His name's Abe," said Teddy.

"Abe?" Dad stood there, shaking his head.

"We can't just shove him out the door," said Tom.

"Jesus, let 'em keep the damn dog," said George.

Abe jumped off the couch and went up to Dad.

Teddy grinned. "Now that we've got an Abe it will be a-okay."

Dad did not lean down and pat Abe on the head. "No, it's not a-okay," he said.

That's when I got mad. I wasn't going to kick our dog out on the street to get hit by a bus or starve to death or get tied up on someone's porch again.

I stood up. Standing made me braver. "Nothing's okay with you," I said. "You could get twenty Abe Lincolns and you'd never be a-okay. He's a happy dog and we need some happy around here." Abe came over and leaned against my legs. I crouched down and gave him a hug. "We're keeping him."

"No, we are not. You had no business dragging that dog home."

Abe jumped back on the couch.

"He's our dog and we're keeping him," I said.

Teddy was crying now and his nose was running. He put his arms around Abe, who licked the snot off his face, which was kind of gross. Tom didn't say anything but he reached over and put his hand on Abe's back.

"Oh hell, stop crying, Teddy." Dad turned and thumped into the kitchen. "You can keep the damn dog."

Chapter 16

Dad didn't say anything about Abe after he gave in and let him stay. He made himself a sandwich, got a beer, sat in his chair, and pretended there wasn't a dog sitting on the couch a couple of feet away.

My stomach was doing flip-flops from standing up for Abe and from the shock of winning. I glanced over at Dad a few times. So did Tom. Dad was chewing his bologna sandwich, ignoring us. But even so I wanted to give him a hug for letting us keep something happy in the house.

After he'd finished his sandwich, Dad looked over at us. "Hey," he said. "It's late. Go to bed."

I smiled. He was up. He was bossing us around. We weren't orphans anymore.

Abe raced upstairs ahead of us.

"I can't believe we get to keep him," said Tom.

"Me neither," I said. "And he got Dad up!"

I read for almost an hour and finished #8. I was really tired but couldn't fall asleep. I rolled over, tried to kick off the covers, and they got tangled around my ankles. I sat up, got untangled, and threw them all on the floor.

Dad was out of bed and we had a dog. Even George had been a good guy for once. But Mom was more gone than before. She had a phone and an apartment. I'd found her but she didn't want to get found. And she'd hung up on me. How can a person just up and decide not to be a mom anymore? I wished George had never told me she'd called him. It had been sad and scary thinking she might be dead but now that I knew she wasn't it was way worse. She was gone on purpose.

I hauled the sheet and blanket off the floor and covered myself up. It didn't matter that it was too hot; it felt safer under the covers. I forced myself to take deep breaths.

Dad thumped up the stairs and down the hall. He was the only one who thumped like that when he walked. "My aching feet are flat but they weren't flat enough to get me out of the army and the Korean War," he'd say, and pop a couple more aspirin.

The toilet flushed and there was more thumping

going back down the stairs. I got up, walked down the hall in the dim light, and sat on the landing. The fridge opened and a beer bottle clinked as Dad wrestled it out of the six-pack. The TV was on—the eleven o'clock news. That wasn't going to cheer him up much. His recliner thunked back and Dad burped. A polite, little burp. I smiled.

"Dad," I called down the stairs.

"Nell? What're you doing up?"

"Can't sleep."

I went downstairs and into the kitchen, got a glass of milk and a couple of Oreos. The sports recap was on. I sat on the couch, dunked one of the Oreos in the milk, and bit off the soft part.

"Damn Red Sox," said Dad. "Lost their lead again."

"Bambino's curse," I said. "Gonna last a hundred years."

"It's a sad thing, that curse," he said, and took a swig of beer. "Boston should have held on to Babe Ruth."

"And the Yankees got him," I said.

"Yeah, that, too. Damn Yankees."

He didn't say a word about disappearing on all of us. Acted like it had never happened. And he didn't mention our new dog, either. Which was a good thing.

The reporter talked about Ehrlichman and Halde-man, who'd worked at the White House and were on trial, and about the secret tape recordings the president had made of all his talks with everyone in the Oval Office. The ads came on and Dad took another swig of beer.

"Why'd the damn fool tape record himself in the first place? That's what I want to know," he said.

I set my glass of milk on the coffee table and studied him. Dad had never in my entire life called President Nixon a damn fool. He hadn't said it in an angry voice. More sad than angry. The president had let Dad down just like Mom and the Red Sox, too.

He lay back in his recliner. The newsman announced that Congress was close to impeaching the president. Dad started repeating, "Damn fool," over and over in the way someone talks about a person they loved who'd screwed up real bad.

"Do you think they'll do it?" I asked.

"Congress is sure gunning for him. If they do it and the Senate convicts him the commies are gonna have a party in Hanoi."

"Oh."

From what I'd seen in the paper and on the news night after night, I figured Nixon really might be a liar and a crook even though he claimed he wasn't. But I didn't argue with Dad because he was awake and downstairs. Abe had worked a miracle and I didn't want to mess that up. Besides, whenever Dad brought up the commies I knew it was a good idea to keep quiet.

The communists and Dad were like the squirrels and Mr. Solano next door. He went crazy over those squirrels raiding his bird feeders—used to sit on his porch taking potshots at them with his BB gun. "Duck and cover, kids," Mom would yell out the window when we were playing outside and the shooting started. "That nutcase is gonna put your eye out. Good thing you've got two each." A couple of months ago Mr. Solano's grown-up daughter had come for a visit and taken his BB gun away. He still hadn't forgiven her.

Dad would take potshots at the commies if he could. President Nixon and Dad felt the same way about the commies as Mr. Solano felt about the squirrels. It seemed like some people became real buddies when they hated the same thing.

Some black-and-white movie about World War II came on. Dad got himself a bowl of pretzels and settled back on his recliner. I drank the last of my milk and smiled. Dad was out of bed and ticked off at the commies again, so things were looking up. He had to leave for work at ten minutes to five in the morning and it was close to midnight but I guessed he'd gotten plenty of sleep already.

"Night, Dad," I said.

"Night, Nellie," he said.

A commercial was on but he still didn't look at me. It had been forever since he'd said, "Sleep tight and don't let the bedbugs bite," which always made me giggle when I was little. Back then I'd imagined bedbugs as these enormous roaches with jaws and real teeth. Now I wished so hard my head ached that he'd say it one more time.

Chapter 17

Boston Herald American, July 19, 1974
"Hush Fund" Transcript Introduced

When I got downstairs Friday morning, Dad's work shoes were missing from the mat by the back door. The whole house seemed to be sucking in the sunlight from outside and I smiled a giant smile, staring down at where his greasy shoes had sat for days.

Abe came running up to say hi.

"Thanks, pup, for getting him out the door," I whispered, giving him a scratch behind his ears where he liked it.

George was in bed. Friday and Saturday were his days off and he never got up before lunchtime. Teddy was watching cartoons. The newspaper was open on the kitchen table so Dad must have looked it over before he left for the Far Reach. The worst news was about President Nixon and his hush fund. He'd paid thousands and thousands of dollars to people so they'd stay quiet about the Watergate break-in and other crimes. He'd hushed them up. Why would he do that if he was innocent?

My horoscope was promising.

Taurus: A fine outlook. Avoid the unconventional, hasty, or erratic, however. You have real opportunity to achieve; don't spoil it through indifference or sporadic effort.

It was a sunny day, Dad was in the world again, and I had a chance to *achieve*, to make a few bucks. Perfect setup for a car wash after lunch. People would want their car clean when they were out shopping or parked in the lot at the temple down on Central Street where the Habermans went or at church on Sunday morning. Not that we went to church or temple or anything, but people got cleaned up if they did. I'd seen the kids in the neighborhood all stiff in their dress-up clothes.

I didn't read Mom's horoscope. I didn't want to know what kind of day she was going to have.

Seventy-four dollars was stuffed in a sock hidden in the pocket of my winter coat in my closet. Three dollars and sixty cents in change from Tom and Carlos was piled on my bureau. South Dakota or bust. I wasn't going to let my stinker of a mom wreck my family. I was going to make a bunch of money with the yard sale, but today I'd start with a car wash.

After.

I went upstairs and pulled ten ones and two five-dollar bills out of the sock for change. Teddy was still watching TV. The kid was going to have mush for brains from sitting so close to the screen. He'd finished his peanut-butter-and-jelly sandwich without me bugging him. Probably gave most of it to Abe.

"Shut it off," I said. "We're gonna wash a bunch of cars."

I opened the basement door.

"Tom?"

"Yeah."

"I need your help."

"I'm gluing the rotor blades."

"I'll give you ten minutes."

I'd seen kids at the high school hold car washes to raise money for band uniforms and class trips. They'd station sign holders on street corners to get customers.

I pulled three sheets of construction paper out of the drawer and made signs:

CAR WASH
$1.00
234 CARLISLE ST.

Tom came up the basement stairs.

"What?" he said.

"I'm doing a car wash. Need your help."

"Sure."

"I need you to hold a sign down on the corner to get customers."

"That's kind of embarrassing."

"Call Carlos. Nothing embarrasses him."

Tom laughed. Last year Carlos had slept over and he'd run all the way to Front Street and back in his underwear when Maya and me bet him a dollar he wouldn't do it. He ran fast, faster on the way back, almost naked, with cars honking at him and people whistling. Maya and me laughed so hard we almost peed in our pants. It had been worth a dollar.

When Carlos showed up today they grabbed two of the signs and took off down the street. Dad had a bucket and sponges and soap under the back steps. I stretched the hose down the driveway past the Dodge Dart that stayed in the driveway since Dad walked to work most days.

Abe was happy in the front yard with his rawhide bone watching us through the chain-link fence. Teddy pulled one of the sponges out of the bucket. "I'll do the hubcaps."

"Great. But for now, stand on the sidewalk and hold the sign up when cars go by."

Our first customer was our next-door neighbor, Mr. Solano. It took him a while to get out of his car with his bad hip. Abe barked and raced around in circles inside the fenced yard.

"Hey, Teddy." Mr. Solano leaned over and gave Teddy a pat on the head. "Got yourself a dog."

"Yup."

"Had a northern flicker at a feeder this morning," said Mr. Solano. "Come over later and I'll show you a picture of it in my bird book."

I brought out a lawn chair so he could sit while we soaped down and rinsed his old car. It was an antique—a Studebaker. Dad said it was worth some money. Teddy was soaking wet by the time he'd finished with the hubcaps and the bumpers and we had two cars waiting in the street.

"Nice job, kids," said Mr. Solano. "Just what I like to see. A little ambition and elbow grease to go with it."

After we washed a couple more cars Mrs. Haberman showed up in her station wagon with the twins in the back seat. She'd rung the doorbell so many times after Mom left I thought Dad might start hiding in the hall closet when he saw her walking up to the house. She was a nice lady. Too nice—always putting on a sad face when she saw me in the street. "How are you, Nellie, dear?"

she'd say like I was going to lie down and die in the next ten minutes.

She sat down in the lawn chair with her pocketbook in her lap and pulled her skirt down over her knees. The twins helped Teddy sponge down the car.

"How's your dad holding up?" Mrs. Haberman asked, slapping on her dopey, sad face.

"He's fine," I said. "At work right now."

I bet Mrs. Haberman watched soap operas every day like Mrs. O'Neill, soaking up all the tragedies that happened to those people on *The Guiding Light* or *As the World Turns*—amnesia, divorce, death, all of it probably made her day. Mom never liked Mrs. Haberman. "That woman's going for perfection. It'll end badly. She'll give herself a heart attack if she ever lets loose a fart in public."

We were busy for a good hour with cars waiting in the street. Nasty Mrs. Longmire pulled her curtains back more times than I could count. After the fifth car backed out of the driveway, clean as a whistle, Carlos and Tom came running down the sidewalk whacking each other on the head with the signs, laughing.

"We're not done yet," I said.

"Boring," said Carlos.

"Yeah, boring and embarrassing," said Tom.

We'd been at it more than an hour and I wasn't going

to push my luck. I'd need the boys again for the car wash I was already planning for next weekend.

"Bring Abe inside, would you?" I said.

Carlos took off for home and Tom used a dog biscuit to get Abe inside the front door. Teddy was still standing on the sidewalk swinging his sign around. An older lady pulled her Ford into the driveway. She got out of her car and smiled at Teddy. I flipped on the sprayer head attached to the hose to wet down the car. That's when Dad showed up, carrying our dinner in a paper bag. It was Friday so it had to be fish sticks.

"What's going on?" he said.

I handed Teddy the hose and turned to talk to Dad.

"NO! Teddy, NO!" Dad yelled.

"Oh my goodness!" screamed the old lady.

When I turned around to look, Teddy, all in a panic, swung the hose away from the open window of her car and sprayed the lady right in the face. I grabbed the hose out of his hand and turned the sprayer off.

"Oops," he said.

The lady was soaked. Water dripped from her hair and face and the whole front of her dress was wet.

"I'm so sorry," I said. "Teddy, get some towels, quick."

I looked in the car window. It was a little damp in the back seat with some puddles on the floor. Dad stood there shaking his head. Across the street Mrs. Longmire pulled her curtain back. I stuck my tongue out at her and she disappeared.

"I'm sorry, ma'am," Dad said, and turned to me. "What the heck are you kids doing?"

"A car wash. To make some money."

"No real harm done," said the lady, laughing. "I'm a lot cooler now."

Teddy came running outside with his arms full of dish towels. I handed one to the lady to dry off, wiped down the back seat of her car, and soaked up the puddles on the floor mats.

"We're gonna wash it for free," I said.

The lady sat down in the lawn chair. "And I'll sit over here where it's safe." She smiled.

Dad mumbled something and went inside. We did a great job on her car and she dug around in her purse and handed me a dollar. Nice lady.

We called it quits after she left. George came home drinking a soda from Nico's Pizza while I was coiling up the hose.

"Hi," said Teddy.

"Hey, squirt," said George. He stepped over the tangled hose and slammed through the back door.

I sat in the lawn chair to count our money while Teddy watched.

"We made six dollars," I said.

"That's a lot."

"Yeah."

I put the bucket with the soap and sponges under the back steps. Teddy held the door for me since I had an armful of soggy towels.

That's when we heard the yelling.

Chapter 18

We stood in the doorway. Teddy pressed his hands over his ears and shook his head, like that would make the shouting stop.

I dumped the wet towels on the floor by the washing machine and walked through the kitchen. Teddy followed close behind. We stopped right inside the living room.

"She didn't steal it!" yelled George.

"How do you know?" yelled Dad.

They were standing just a couple of feet apart, Dad still in his greasy work clothes. George was almost as tall as him. Skinnier, but at that moment he looked stronger and like a grown-up man.

"I just know, okay?" said George.

"She'd take it in a heartbeat," said Dad, quieter now. "Walked out on all you kids. What would stop her from stealing?"

"Walked out on you, not us," said George, under his breath.

"How would you know?"

"She said so. Couldn't stay in this house with you another day."

Tom came up from the basement and stood next to me. Abe squeezed up against Teddy, almost knocking him over. We didn't move, stuck in that spot like we had glue on the soles of our sneakers.

"You talked to her?" Dad moved a step closer. George backed up.

"Yeah. She called and I talked to her."

Dad stood there, frozen. I knew how he felt—the shock of it when George told me about Mom. There was a long, long silence. Dad stared at George like he was a person he'd only just met.

"I took the money." George stood up straight and stuck out his chest like a kid on the playground making a dare. "She said she needed it and I gave it to her."

Right that second Dad should have run up the stairs, gotten into bed, and pulled the covers over his head.

But he didn't.

He shoved George.

With both hands, Dad pushed hard on George's chest. "You little weasel," he yelled. George's right leg buckled and he tipped sideways. Dad pushed him again. "Thieving snake."

George fell backward. He landed hard. His head thumped on the floor.

Dad moved forward and leaned down. "Get out of my house. Go find your precious mother."

George scrambled backward, pushing on the floor with his hands. "She hates you," he said loud and hard.

"Get out. NOW! I don't want to see your damn face."

Dad turned and climbed the stairs. Teddy crouched down, his arms around Abe. George's face was red and his eyes were watering. Tears. Tears dripped off his chin.

"Dad's not the one who left." I said it low and soft. I hated George for what he'd done but he was crying. George crying. And Dad had knocked him down.

And Tom was crying, too. And Teddy. But I was too mad at George. At Dad. At Mom. Too mad to cry.

George wiped his face and stood up, a foot taller than me. His tears were gone. He glared at me. "Mom finding a place to live's more important than all of you gawking at a bunch of rocks on some mountain."

"She's got a place to live. Right here," I said.

"She couldn't live here. Not anymore." George

looked over at Tom and Teddy and Abe. "And I guess I can't, either."

"He didn't mean it," said Tom.

"I don't care if he meant it or not. He said it."

George climbed the stairs and we all stood there in the living room not talking, not moving. Teddy was crying hard with lots of sniffling while Abe licked his face.

"Bring your crayons and stuff in here," I said.

Tom wiped his face with his sleeve. "Do you think he's really gonna leave?"

"I don't care," I said.

But I didn't mean it. George was never all that nice and he'd gotten meaner since Mom left. But seeing him sitting on his butt, crying, he looked like a first grader who'd tripped and fallen on the playground. For a moment I wanted to hug him like I used to when I was little. I used to run up and give him a hug when he came home from school and he'd push me away but I tried over and over anyway. George was my big brother, who could be a real jerk but I still didn't want him to leave.

Tom kicked at Dad's recliner. "This family sucks!"

"Yeah," I said.

Tom turned and disappeared into the kitchen and down to the basement and the hundreds of plastic parts, brushes, and decals. Teddy came in with his box of crayons and coloring book and sat on the couch with me and

Abe. I picked up Nancy Drew #9 and gripped it with both hands. It was solid and the pages were numbered all in order. One then two then three, so there was no way to get lost.

George came banging down the stairs carrying a duffle bag. I closed my book, holding my place with my thumb. Teddy clutched his black crayon stub like it would save him from drowning or something.

"I'll be at Glenn's," said George.

He didn't wait for an answer, didn't wait for me to say, "Don't go." He just slammed through the door.

I could hear the shower going upstairs. The air in the house was muggy thick. My head hurt along with a panicky choking ache in my chest. Teddy put his crayon stub in its place in the box. He looked up at me like I'd have something helpful to say.

"Keep going," I said.

He pulled out the taped blue-violet crayon, leaned over his coloring book, and began on the sky. I curled up on the couch holding my book. Abe put his head on my feet. I wished I knew everything was going to turn out all fine and dandy like in Nancy's life. But it wasn't.

At four I turned on the TV. It was too quiet in the house after the yelling. Teddy went and sat on the floor a couple of feet from the screen with Abe. A couple of feet away from Mr. Rogers. Tom came upstairs and sat on the couch. He didn't try to change the channel.

We watched together. Mr. Rogers talked about the fish in his fish tank while he fed them. He was such a nice person. And I was certain he'd be that way if I met him on the street, just him. It didn't really matter what he was saying on the TV. His voice stitched up the seams on the falling-apart baseball that was my world right then.

But when he put his button-up sweater on, changed his shoes, and said goodbye, George and Mom were gone again.

It helped that Tom and Teddy were there in the living room. The three of us together. We all watched some nature show about elephants and we even laughed when the baby elephant ran between the legs of its mom when it got frightened by some bird.

I heated up the fish sticks and fries from the Far Reach for dinner. Dad thumped downstairs and sat in his recliner. I guess he didn't have to hide in his room cooling off his temper. He'd used it up when he knocked George down and kicked him out of the house. He didn't bring it up. I kept quiet. So did Tom and Teddy.

We needed Mom there to make some crack about Dad and George. To say it out loud: "Knocking your kids around now, huh, Ronnie?" It wouldn't matter if she made things worse, like always, since everything was so rotten already. At least if someone did some talking the air in the house wouldn't be so thick and dark.

We ate dinner while we watched the six o'clock news. When *I Dream of Jeannie* came on Dad didn't chuckle like he usually did. No one laughed out loud even when Jeannie got mad and turned her husband into a rooster.

I studied my brothers and Dad, their eyes glued to the TV. George was gone. It wasn't like he ever hung around the house on Friday nights, but we all knew he wouldn't be banging through the door close to midnight, waking everyone up. We *were* scared little bunnies, even Dad. At least George said things out loud like Mom. Me and what was left of my family didn't say a word. We just sat there watching a comedy show with any laughter as far away as the moon.

Chapter 19

Boston Herald American, July 20, 1974
*Special Counsel Calls for
Nixon Impeachment*

Saturday morning I got up after Dad left for work. I got the yard sale signs out of the hall closet and set them on the kitchen table. I was too nervous to eat. Selling Mom's stuff was going to get me in a bunch of trouble with Dad and even worse trouble if Mom found out. And selling her stuff was kind of like me kicking what was left of her out of the house. The whole thing was a terrible idea. But not going on our trip would be worse for everyone who was left.

I flipped the signs over and opened the day's paper. The front page was more bad news for President Nixon. He hadn't handed over all the secret tapes. But he did turn over most of them and the newspaper had printed what he'd said on page two. Nixon called loads of people sons of you-know-whats right in the Oval Office. Not very presidential. Kind of dumb, too. If I knew I was being recorded, I'd watch my language.

My horoscope was mysterious today:

> **Taurus: If you do not notice "small" errors and where you miss chances for "little" gains, you will probably not see the big ones. Be alert.**

I guessed I'd better pay attention during the yard sale—price everything right and be on the lookout for people pocketing stuff without paying. I sure hoped the *big gains* part was going to happen. Mom's horoscope said she was gonna have a somewhat mild day. That's exactly what drove her nuts, the mildness of her life. No excitement, just one sink full of dishes after another. Maybe her new life didn't fix anything. Maybe she just found herself a different bucket of mildness somewhere else. It would serve her right.

Maya showed up at seven with sheets of orange stickers and her mom's change box.

"Your dad's at work?"

I told her about George and Dad and the fight.

"Holy moley! He hit him?"

"Pushed him. Hard."

"Where'd he go?"

"Glenn's."

Maya fiddled with a sheet of orange stickers.

"You sure about this?" she said.

"Yeah, I'm sure."

Maya was quiet, stared at me.

"No," I said. "I'm not sure. But I'm gonna do it anyway."

We carried a roll of duct tape and the signs we'd made into the living room. Teddy was lying on the rug with Abe, watching TV.

"Hey," I said. "We're going for a quick walk. Did you feed the dog?"

He nodded, not taking his eyes off *The Road Runner*.

We taped signs up on telephone poles around the neighborhood. Only ten of them, but Maya said that was plenty.

Back at the house we went down to the basement. Dozens of Tom's model planes hung on fishing line tied to the water pipes in the ceiling. We got the air moving as we walked and the planes started a slow spin, making me dizzy.

Behind Tom's table, the wall was covered in gray metal shelving. A whole section was filled with camping gear. All last year, every time Dad had some spare cash, he'd drive down to the Army/Navy Surplus Store in Davis Square. He had everything ready for our big road trip—canvas tents, a huge cooler, sleeping bags, a cook stove.

He'd packed the liquor boxes labeled CONNIE on

two shelves in the corner. Maya grabbed the first box and handed it to me. I got a green canvas tarp off the shelf with the camping gear, took a deep breath, and headed up the stairs.

Our driveway ran up along the fence enclosing the front yard. We didn't have a garage like some of the houses on the block. Dad's Dodge Dart was parked next to the side door that led into the kitchen. We spread the tarp out on the driveway close to the sidewalk. By eight o'clock we'd carried all the boxes outside.

"One more thing," I said.

My red Schwinn was leaning up against the wall by the furnace in the basement. I wrestled it upstairs and rolled it through the kitchen and out to the driveway.

"Not your bike!" said Maya.

"Why not? Can't ride it anymore. My knees bump. What do you think? Fifteen bucks?"

"Jeesh, Nellie. You love that bike."

I ignored her, set the kickstand, and parked the bike on the tarp.

"Okay, it's your yard sale," said Maya. "We better tag everything or they'll haggle too much."

"My horoscope warned me about details like that," I said.

Maya rolled her eyes. "We need hangers."

I ran back into the house and up the stairs. The

closet in Dad's room was sad. His one suit he'd worn to Fannie's daughter's wedding was hanging there, and a few shirts, but it was mostly empty with tons of mismatched hangers on the pole where Mom's clothes used to be. I grabbed the hangers and headed downstairs.

Teddy looked up from a commercial. "What're you doing?" he said.

"Trying to make some more money for our trip."

"Oh."

Mr. Magoo came on and he turned back to the TV.

Back outside I dumped the hangers on the tarp and yanked open a box. The smell was like a slap—a muddle of baby powder and hair spray and cigarettes. The smell of my mom. Breathing it in made me want to throw up again.

I kicked the box.

"You sure you wanna do this?" said Maya. "Mom can't get rid of Stefan's stuff. Probably never will."

We stood there and stared at all the boxes. Maya's older brother, Stefan, had died in Vietnam two years ago. A booby trap on one of those trails in the jungle. Stefan always used to give me a stick of Wrigley's spearmint gum out of the pack he kept in his shirt pocket. "Here you go, kid," he'd say. Maya told me her mom still cries. In the middle of making breakfast or vacuuming she'll start crying and then Maya starts crying, too.

"Let's get this over with," I said.

People showed up way before nine. We had all Mom's dresses and skirts and blouses and coats on hangers strung along the chain-link fence. Maya kept the jewelry next to the cash box so she could keep an eye on it. Everything else we laid out on the tarp.

It was my mom, in pieces, for sale—her sewing box with the pincushion shaped like a pumpkin, the fuzzy blue coat she wore when it was really cold, her snow boots with the pom-poms on the ends of the laces. It was even harder than I thought it would be.

The fourth customer bought my red Schwinn bike. Maya helped her load it in the back seat of her car. I shouldn't have cared since I couldn't use it, but I did. I loved those tassels, how they flew out beside me when I picked up speed.

Tom showed up right after the lady drove off with my bike. He stood at the end of the driveway staring at all of Mom's stuff.

He walked over and picked up Mom's sewing box and pulled out the pincushion.

"What are you doing?"

"We're selling it all so we can go on the trip."

He put the pincushion back and gripped the box with both hands. "Okay. But I'm keeping this."

"Sure," I said.

142

He didn't even know how to thread a needle but that box had been on the shelf in the living room forever. We'd poke around in it, steal buttons for game pieces, bring it to Mom when she had to sew a patch on our jeans or needed a needle to dig a splinter out of one of our fingers. She'd touched everything in there over and over. I understood why he wanted it. Why he was holding on to it so tight. It was filled up with Mom.

Most of the morning I stood by the fence with my hands in my pockets while Maya made change. People tried to bargain. Mrs. Carmine bought three dresses and tried to get Maya to throw in Mom's black silk blouse she wore to funerals.

"Gotta pay what it says on the tag," said Maya.

Mrs. Carmine clicked her tongue and paid up.

By ten we'd sold about half the clothes and almost all the jewelry. I wasn't sure we charged enough for the jewelry since people snapped it up. But it's not like it was real gold or loaded with Elizabeth Taylor diamonds.

Mrs. Longmire kept an eye on us through her front window. Neighbors came by and bought stuff but gave us funny looks. Some were suspicious.

"You sure your mother won't be back for her things?"

"Your dad gave you the okay for this, right?"

I nodded and put on a sad face, which usually shut them up, but mostly I let Maya handle the questions. I knew that she knew I was close to falling to pieces, since she kept giving me looks, waiting for me to say let's stop this now.

It quieted down around eleven. Tom came outside with his baseball glove.

"See you," I said. He nodded. It wasn't an angry nod. More like an I-don't-want-to-have-anything-to-do-with-all-this nod.

I ran inside and got a couple of glasses of Kool-Aid and Maya and me sat in the beat-up lawn chairs we'd dragged off the back porch and took a break. Teddy came out, still in his pj's. He closed the gate behind him to keep Abe in the yard. When he got to the end of the driveway, Teddy eyed the jewelry that was left on the tarp.

"That's Mom's sunflower pin," he said, pointing to a cheesy pin she must have bought with her discount at work.

"Yeah," I said.

"Why's it out here?"

Right then Mrs. Longmire showed up in her ugly housedress and stood at the end of the driveway with her hands on her hips.

"You should be ashamed of yourself, Nellie Sanders. Selling all your mother's belongings when she could be lying dead in a gutter somewhere."

Teddy's eyes went wide. He reached down and grabbed the sunflower pin.

"It's none of your business what I do," I said.

"Did *she* put you up to this?" Mrs. Longmire pointed at Maya. She didn't like kids whose parents came from the Azores or black kids or Dominicans. On Halloween she wouldn't answer the door if any of *those* kids were standing on her stoop in their costumes.

"What're you getting at?" I said, sitting up in my chair.

"Does that father of yours know what you're doing?" Mrs. Longmire stepped closer.

Teddy stood there, barefoot, in his pj's, gripping the sunflower pin so tight his fingers had gone all splotchy pink. He looked up at me waiting for an answer.

Mrs. Longmire stood there, too, her mouth in a mean grin, happy about the trouble she was stirring up.

"I'm starving," said Maya. "You two go make us some sandwiches. I'll keep an eye on things." She sat back in her lawn chair, legs crossed, arms folded across her chest, and started a staring contest with Mrs. Longmire.

I grinned. Couldn't help it. That was Maya—a tough cookie in her shorts and T-shirt taking on the nosiest, nastiest old lady in the neighborhood.

"Well, I never." Mrs. Longmire gave one big "humph" and marched across the street to her house.

"Way to go," I said. "Come on, Teddy."

In the kitchen I got the grape jelly out of the fridge.

"Is Mom dead? Is that why you're selling her clothes?" Teddy stood by the table still holding the sunflower pin in his fist.

"No, silly. She's not dead. I'm selling her old stuff so we can go on our trip."

"Oh." Teddy stared down at the pin in the palm of his hand.

"You can't tell Dad," I said. "It's a secret."

"But what's Mom gonna wear now?"

I laid out six slices of bread on the counter. "She'll buy more clothes at the store."

"Oh."

"Hey, what're you still doing in your pj's? Go get dressed and meet me outside."

Teddy went upstairs and I finished making the sandwiches. When I got outside there were a couple of people going through the paperbacks.

"Six for a dollar," said Maya, still in her lawn chair.

A woman picked up Mom's favorite green sweater. It was way too big but in the winter Mom wore it when she sat on the couch with her legs stretched out reading one of her mysteries.

Seeing that lady touch Mom's sweater got me in a crazy panic.

"THAT'S NOT FOR SALE!" I yelled.

The two women and Maya stared at me.

"Sorry, sorry," I said. "It's just that I didn't mean to put that out here."

"Okay, honey," said the woman, handing me the sweater. "No problem."

Maya didn't say anything about the sweater after they left. I draped it over the back of my chair and sat down. A couple of Mom's bangle bracelets were still left in the pile of jewelry. I picked them up and stashed them in my pocket.

"We can stop, now," said Maya. "A hundred and twenty-seven bucks so far."

"No, it's okay." I tried to smile. That was a ton of money. But most of Mom's things were gone now, carried off into the neighborhood, hung up in other people's closets. I couldn't take any of it back.

Teddy ran outside and flopped down on the tarp. We ate our sandwiches. It was hot and muggy and I had a sunburn on my nose and my arms. We had a few more customers but there wasn't much left to sell. Dad's shift ended at two and we had to have everything cleared out before he got home.

We packed what was left into a couple of boxes and carried them inside. Teddy set himself up at the kitchen table with his coloring book and Maya got him a glass of milk. Abe curled up under the table.

"Be back real soon," I said.

We ran around the neighborhood, pulled down the yard sale signs and jammed them into a garbage can outside the liquor store three blocks from the house. When we got back we were both sweaty and hot. Maya carried empty boxes inside while I went upstairs and put Mom's green sweater and the bangles in my bottom drawer.

Once I'd hung the empty hangers back in Dad's closet and we'd stacked the mostly empty boxes with CONNIE written on the sides on the shelves in the basement, the yard sale might never have happened.

I shoved the tarp back on the shelf with Dad's camping gear. Tom's model airplanes spun in circles over my head. The smell of my mom—her hairspray, baby powder, cigarettes—was sucked out of the house now, except the bit of it on her green sweater in my bottom drawer.

"Gotta go," Maya yelled down the basement stairs. "My mom's gonna send out the National Guard searching for me."

I didn't answer. Barely heard her.

She came down the stairs. "You did it."

"Yeah," I said.

Maya came over and put her arms around me. She

didn't squeeze me tight, just held on to me for a while. It made it easier to breathe. She let go and backed up a few feet, looked up at the planes spinning over our heads.

"And here." She dug a wad of bills out of her back pocket and shoved it in my hand. "Thirty-seven bucks. All I've got. You can pay me back after you've checked all those new states off your list."

"Thanks." I hardly got the word out trying to hold back the tears.

"Come over later," Maya said. "I gotta go or I'm grounded for life."

I climbed the stairs and stood in the doorway to the kitchen. Teddy had managed to attach Mom's sunflower pin to his T-shirt. It sagged, almost upside-down on the flimsy material. He gripped his gray crayon tight while he colored in the street under the Batmobile.

We'd hidden all the evidence. But the problem was that half the neighborhood knew about the yard sale. I wasn't too worried about Mrs. Longmire since she hadn't spoken to Dad in ages. Not since he told her she was a mean old bigot for not giving candy to *all* the kids on Halloween. "You deserve a lot worse than getting your sorry old rosebushes wrapped up in toilet paper," he'd said.

But everyone loved to gossip and my secret yard sale wasn't exactly under wraps. Maybe if Dad walked home with a big dark cloud hovering over his head like usual, people would stay away from him, keep their mouths shut. Maybe.

Chapter 20

Dad got home a little after two, took his shower, and settled into his recliner with his newspaper. After a gloomy "Hey, kids," he didn't say a word. Nothing about George. Nothing about Mom taking the money. Nothing.

"I'm going over to Maya's," I said.

"Sure," he mumbled from behind his paper.

My job watching Teddy was done once Dad got home but I was sure glad Abe was there to keep an eye on him. When I got outside I noticed that Mr. Solano had put the flag up on his front porch. Since his daughter took away his BB gun he'd been using old tennis balls to keep the squirrels off his bird feeders. He had a pretty good throwing arm for an old guy with a bad hip. When he'd pitched all the balls at the squirrels he'd put the flag up. Teddy would go over and run around his yard and crawl under the bushes to collect them. Each time he filled up the laundry basket with tennis balls and delivered it to Mr. Solano on his porch he earned a dime.

I went back into the house and Teddy looked up from his coloring book.

"Flag's flying. Better get to work. Leave Abe in the front yard."

He pulled his cap on and ran out the front door. Abe raced after him. I left out the back door and walked up the block.

It would have been great to have grandparents like old Mr. Solano, but Dad's parents died before Teddy was even born. I hardly remembered them. Our house used to be theirs. Our family lived with them until they died. Mom called it the "sardine years" since the house was packed with kids and adults like sardines in a can. Mom's parents moved to Florida when I was five and they'd never called or even sent cards for birthdays or anything. "I hope their morning glasses of Florida orange juice give them heartburn," Mom said. I figured I was lucky they were far away.

A bunch of boys, younger than me, were playing street hockey on Eliot Ave. I knew most of them from school. They were screaming bloody murder as they banged their hockey sticks on the pavement.

"Here! Tony! Pass it!"

"Block him, Oscar!"

"Guido, you bonehead. Pass it, would ya?"

Tony slammed the puck down the street toward the goal, which was marked out by two garbage cans. When it slowed down I could tell it wasn't a real hockey puck or a rubber ball. It was a bald, one-eyed doll's head, her nose squashed flat, rolling in a lopsided zigzag, ending up under a parked van.

"What's with the puck?" I asked Oscar.

"Best ever," he said, grinning at me while Guido crawled under the van. "We never lose it 'cause the ears slow it down."

"Got it!" yelled Guido from under the van. The doll's head rolled out into the street and the rest of them chased after it. I laughed. Before she became a hockey puck that doll probably got tucked into bed by some little girl who loved her. It was too gruesome.

A car horn honked, then another. A line of traffic was jammed up by the game. Tony and Oscar moved the garbage cans so the cars could get through. I kept walking.

The bell tied to the frame jingled when I pulled open the heavy door to Manny's Convenience. Mrs. Machado was sweeping the aisle between two high shelves stacked with canned goods, coffee, bread, and everything anyone needed in a hurry.

"Nellie, mi querida," she said, leaning the broom against the shelf.

Mrs. Machado opened her arms and waited. Her hug didn't last long since we were both hot and sweaty. I stepped back and got some distance between us.

"Get yourself a soda," she said, motioning to the glass-fronted refrigerator case. "This heat."

I pulled a bottle of root beer out of the case. The cool air washed over me.

"How's your papa?"

"Okay."

I glanced down the aisle toward the back entrance to the stairs to their apartment. "Maya here?"

"Just went up."

Halfway up the stairs I could hear David Cassidy's voice singing, "I Think I Love You." Maya never let me talk when he was singing. I was surprised her Partridge Family cassette hadn't worn out, the tape rubbed clean. Ugh.

I took a sip of root beer and opened the door at the top of the stairs. The Machado apartment was crammed with heavy furniture, framed photos on the walls, and the smell of lemon and spices and fish. It was dark since all the shades were down to keep out the heat.

On a low table against the wall was an altar with a statue of Saint Anthony and electric candles glowing red on either side. Maya's grandfather's chair by the window was empty. He was probably at the park playing dominoes with the other old guys.

I stood there drinking my soda, waiting for David Cassidy to shut up. One of the red bulbs by the altar blinked on and off like it was sending a message in Morse code. Maybe that's how saints communicated now there was electricity. Finally the song was over and I hurried down the hall before it started up again.

The door to Maya and her sister Marta's room was open. Marta was sixteen and worked full-time at the new McDonald's in Porter Square for the summer.

"Hey," I said. "You done with Davey-Boy?"

"Torture's over," she said. "How ya doing?"

I plunked down on Marta's bed. The room was tiny but neat. Mrs. Machado was strict that way, too. Maya was staring into a hand mirror, her eyelids flickering as she loaded on blue eye shadow. She'd changed her clothes since the yard sale—shorts and a tank top with a blouse over it.

"I have a date," she said, still not looking at me.

"A date?" I stared at her. "What do you mean a date?"

"With Joey."

"He's sixteen or something!"

"So?"

I studied her—perfect long black hair, hoop earrings, bracelets. Maya'd turned into Alien Maya in just a couple of hours. Was it David Cassidy and "I Think I Love You" drilling into her skull every second?

A bunch of times this summer we'd met up with Paul and Mika at Nico's Pizza on Cambridge Street. But it was mostly by accident when we ran into them and the boys always acted like clowns, getting tomato sauce on their shirts and horsing around with the hot-pepper flakes. We were all in the same grade so it wasn't much different from eating at the same table at the cafeteria at school. It sure wasn't a date.

And how was she going to go on a date without her mom finding out and locking her up in her room for the rest of the summer?

"How're you gonna get away with this?" I said.

"I told Mom I'd be at your house."

"If she finds out, you're so dead. And he's too old."

Alien Maya put the tiny brush back in the blue eye shadow case and gave me a look like she didn't know me anymore, either.

"You my mother now?"

She said it in her truly mean voice. The one she used at school when she was telling off some eighth grader giving us a hard time. The one she used when she talked about Mr. Ponti, our social studies teacher, who was all rah-rah about the war in Vietnam. The war that killed Stefan. She used that voice on me.

"No," I said. "I'm not your mother."

"Sure sounds like it."

"Even George says Joey's a jerk."

"He is not." She jammed her makeup bag under her pillow. "And you're stuck back in elementary school. Freaked out just trying on a bra. Grow up, why don't you."

I wanted to slap her. I wanted to pop precious David Cassidy out of the cassette player and stomp on him.

In the last week of school, Maya and her sister had ganged up on me to try on a bra. Marta sat on her bed, made me stand up straight, and inspected my tiny boobs hidden under my T-shirt.

"Not much there, but you're ready," she'd said.

My face had gone red as a fire truck and I'd pulled my shoulders forward to hide my chest. Maya had handed me one of her first bras. Ordered me to put it on. In the bathroom down the hall I'd wrestled with the thing and when I came back they'd given me the once-over.

"Don't exactly fill it up, do you?" Marta said.

The Machado family was packed with women and girls. Maya's dad worked at the rubber hose factory on the day shift while her mom ran the store. At night, Mr. Machado took over at the store, eating his dinner between sales of cigarettes and milk. So it was all girls pretty much all the time. Carmina, the oldest daughter, was living in Boston now in an apartment with more girls. Going to nursing school.

I'd never noticed all the Machado girlness when me and Maya were in elementary school running around in flip-flops and cut-off jeans, before Alien Maya started showing up, changing her clothes three times a day, wearing makeup, and now going on real dates.

I glared at her. "I may be stuck in elementary school but at least I haven't gotten stupid. Boy stupid. David Cassidy stupid. Joey stupid."

"Grow up!" she yelled.

I walked out then. I thought about giving Maya back her thirty-seven dollars I still had in my back pocket but I didn't. I got up off the bed and walked out of Maya's room, stomped down the stairs and through the store. Mrs. Machado was making change for some guy buying a bag of chips and a soda. She gave me a big smile. I gave her a fake one back.

"Leaving already?" she asked.

"Yeah," I said. "Thanks for the soda."

My T-shirt was stuck to my sweaty back. And my bra, the one I'd inherited from Maya, was damp and grabbed me tight around the chest, making it hard to breathe. I wanted to take back a lot of what I'd said. I was the Alien, not Maya. I was the weirdo who loved the wrong music and lived in a house filled up with Huey Helicopters, Batman and Robin, and dead presidents.

I stopped walking, stood there on Benton Street outside the Laundromat. I was caught between the hot sun bombarding me from above and the heat of the pavement rising up, roasting me like a chicken. Sweat dripped off my chin. I didn't want to go home. I wanted to go back, sit on Marta's bed. Tell Maya I was sorry. Really sorry. I would let her doll me up with all her makeup, paint my toenails, even pierce my ears like she'd been begging to do for months.

But I'd just be faking it. Maya was no dummy. I couldn't sit there and honest-to-God swoon over David Cassidy and the new lipstick she'd just gotten at Walgreens. We'd just start fighting again, especially if Maya really did go on a date with stupid Joey.

A bus drove by stinking up the air. Some kid started crying in the Laundromat. I looked in the big window.

A little girl was strapped down in a stroller, screaming. Her face was red and she was pointing. Her mom leaned down and picked up a pink plastic pony with a blond tail and gave it to the kid. She quieted down, clutched that stupid pony tight against her chest.

Right there on the street I was close to bawling like that kid. I wanted to sit down on the sidewalk and cry my eyes out. And a pink plastic pony wouldn't help me any. Probably make me cry harder.

Chapter 21

When I got home from Maya's I didn't say hi to Teddy lying on the rug with Abe watching TV. I walked right by Dad in his recliner, went straight up the stairs to my room. I wanted to kick that idiot pink pony over a cliff.

It was even hotter upstairs. I yanked my sweaty T-shirt off, wrestled out of Maya's old bra, and pulled on a clean shirt, a baggy one, so my tiny boobs didn't show. All the hippie girls in Harvard Square and the Boston Common and loads of college students I'd seen walking around didn't believe in bras. It was all about women's liberation. Mom had said, "I missed the liberation boat. Won't let you get on board with four kids and dirty dishes in the sink." I don't think we stopped her from being a women's libber. She wasn't brave enough. She just ran away.

Those girls with no bras seemed really happy—their boobs bounced around all free because they'd gotten out of bra jail. Well, I wasn't going to wear one, either. It wasn't like I was going to stand out in a crowd as a women's liberation girl since no one could probably tell the difference. But I'd know.

I pulled Maya's thirty-seven dollars out of my back pocket and got the sock with the car-wash money and the yard sale money and my stereo money out of the pocket of my winter coat in the closet. I dumped all of it onto my bed, flattened out the bills, and organized the coins in piles of a dollar. When I was done I grabbed the two bucks I'd made gardening for the O'Neills and the three dollars and sixty cents in change from Tom and Carlos off my bureau and added it to the piles. All together I had two hundred fifty-four dollars and eighty-seven cents.

I'd earn thirty bucks watching Teddy before we had to leave and probably spend five of it on subway rides, but that still left twenty-five bucks. That meant no ice cream when the truck drove by tinkling its bell. No movies or pizza or anything that cost money. I had less than three weeks to scrape together two hundred and twenty-one bucks. I'd made a mess out of having a best friend, so I'd have to do it without Maya. Which was going to be a lot harder.

And George was gone. Were we going to get in Dad's car and drive off, leaving him at Glenn's? The trip was supposed to make our family a family again. It was supposed to fill Dad's heart back up with hope once he saw his mountain. We were supposed to sit around a campfire in brand-new states, all five of us, six counting Abe. Together.

If we went without George it would be like shining a spotlight on him being missing along with Mom already gone. Driving west without George calling shotgun, fighting with Dad about which radio station to listen to, was not going to make anything better. Even though he was a pain in the neck, he had to be in that car with us.

I stuffed the money in the sock and put it back in the pocket of my coat in the closet. I wanted to call Maya and say I was sorry and meet her for pizza at Nico's. But I was still mad at her and she was probably still mad at me. And I'd already decided I couldn't run around spending the Rushmore money on things like pizza.

I grabbed #9 off my bedside table, went downstairs and out to the backyard. Mr. Solano was sitting on his porch watching his birds. He'd rigged up wires and tin-foil hats on the feeders, but the squirrels always figured out a way to steal the birdseed. They were like Olympic athletes the way they hung upside down or leaped from a branch to a pole to a wire.

"Hi," I said from my side of the fence.

"Hello, Nellie," he said, waving.

"Do you have any weeding or yard work that needs doing?"

"Might have. What do you charge?"

"By the job," I said.

For a couple of hours I weeded, raked, edged the lawn around his driveway, and swept out his garage. Mr. Solano was an easy boss. He gave me a price, told me what to do, and didn't hover like Mr. O'Neill. When I'd put the rake and edger back in his garage and met him on the porch, he handed me a glass of lemonade with ice in it along with four bucks.

"Thanks," I said.

"It'll be easier for Teddy to find the tennis balls now," he said, studying his backyard.

I liked Mr. Solano. After Mom left he didn't give me sad looks like the rest of them did every time I walked down the street. Mrs. Solano had died years and years ago and his daughter had gotten married, so he was alone. But he loved his birds. Teddy did, too—he'd sit on Mr. Solano's porch with him and watch the birds for ages. At night, out our kitchen window, I could see the bluish light of his TV and hear him laugh at some show or other through his open window—laughing all by himself.

"So, Nellie," he said. "Why do elephants paint their toenails red, green, blue, yellow, and orange?" He started laughing before I could even answer. Mr. Solano knew at least a thousand elephant jokes. Teddy loved them but never told them right when he came home from tennis ball duty or bird watching.

"Why?" I said, smiling. A person couldn't help smiling around Mr. Solano.

"So they can hide in a bag of M&M's."

"Oh jeez, that's really bad," I said, laughing.

"Isn't it? Just awful." Mr. Solano giggled. I swear, he giggled like a little kid. Then his face got serious. "George will come home, you know. I can tell you're a worrier. He'll be back."

"Did Teddy tell you?" I said.

"Yes. And I heard the ruckus the other day. He'll be back. George is sixteen. He's trying to figure things out."

"Problem is he already thinks he's figured everything out."

"That's part of being sixteen, too." Mr. Solano shook his head like he was thinking back on when he was a teenager. "Hey," he said, grinning. "Why did the Boy Scout fall flat on his face?"

"Why?"

"He tried to carry a bag of M&M's home. Get it?" He laughed again, his head back, hooting at the sky.

"That's even stupider!" I said, and laughed out loud because Mr. Solano was hooting and stamping his good foot on the deck.

When I got inside, Teddy was on the floor with Abe, working on his coloring book. Dad was in his chair asleep.

"Want to hear a stupid joke?" I said.

"Okay," he said.

I had to explain about the elephant in the bag of M&M's. Teddy giggled and I laughed at what a dumb joke it was even though I didn't believe Mr. Solano. I didn't think George was coming back.

Chapter 22

Boston Herald American, July 21, 1974
The Tangled Case of Watergate:
Where It Now Stands

I slept late Sunday morning. When I got downstairs, the boys were half watching the cartoons while Tom read the Sunday comics out loud.

"Get dressed," I said. "Gotta go."

Sunday morning we always walked to the Far Reach for breakfast. I stuffed my school bag with Teddy's crayons, coloring book, and #9. We left Abe in the kitchen with his rawhide bone and the doors closed. He liked it under the table.

We'd done this forever. Every Sunday morning Mom would shove us out the door. "I need some peace and quiet. Go get your pancakes," she'd say.

Once when I was in fourth grade I'd stayed behind,

waited on the couch, pretending to read Encyclopedia Brown.

"What're you still doing here?" Mom said, standing in the doorway, a cigarette in her right hand, the smoke snaking up toward the ceiling.

"I want to stay here with you," I'd said.

"If you're looking for mother-daughter time this is not the moment," Mom said, and took a drag on her cigarette. "Get going."

Her words hurt, like a spray of hot sparks burning holes in the picture in my head of me and Mom curled up at either end of the couch reading our mysteries.

I never tried it again.

The three of us stopped at the Morettis' house. Jack barked while Mr. Moretti sat in his chair puffing on his cigar. Mrs. Moretti hated those cigars and wouldn't let him smoke inside. And Jack hated us. He hated anybody who got near his house. Especially the postman. Teddy waved and Mr. Moretti nodded.

Tom found a Pepsi can in the gutter and kicked it down the sidewalk ahead of us. Teddy kept stopping to inspect some ants or pick up a soda pop pull tab and shove it in his pocket. I didn't mind taking our time since my head hurt from thinking about Mom and because I wasn't sure if George would be there working. Did he quit his job to avoid Dad? Did Dad get Lou to fire him?

I didn't want to talk to George but I did want to see him so I didn't keep wondering if he was okay.

Tom gave the can one last kick into the street and we went in. Fannie was at the cash register by the door. She had on her blue waitress dress and a white apron. "Kids are here, Ronnie!" she hollered. Teddy made to run past her but she grabbed him by the shoulders and gave him a wet kiss on the cheek while he shut his eyes and went all stiff like he was getting electrocuted.

"How's my sweet Teddykins?" she asked, holding him in place.

"Okay," he said, scrubbing at the lipstick on his cheek with his fist.

Tom was next. Fannie squashed his head against her chest. Half his face was visible and he gave me a look out of his free eye like he might be dying. I tried not to laugh.

When she hugged me Fannie whispered in my ear, "How're you doing, honey?"

I mumbled, "Is George here?"

"He's here," she said. "Pigheaded, the pair of 'em. Haven't said a word to each other all morning."

"Hey, Fannie," someone called from a booth. "Where's my refill?"

"Hold your horses, Bennie."

She went behind the counter for the coffeepot, and me and the boys hurried to our regular booth in the

169

far corner and slid into our seats. Teddy was still scrubbing at the lipstick on his face. Fannie had started with the hugs and kisses after Mom left. "You poor motherless darlings," she'd said. It wasn't exactly true since our mother wasn't dead, just gone.

I got up, slipped behind the counter, and filled three glasses with orange juice at the big dispenser and brought them back to the table. Teddy dug around in my book bag for his crayons and coloring book and Tom pulled a comic book out of his back pocket. With George in the kitchen I knew I wasn't going to be able to concentrate on #9 so I sat and watched Fannie move up and down the counter, refilling coffee mugs, chatting with her regulars.

I could see the top half of Dad in the kitchen through the opening in the back of the counter where he set plates of food. He wore his Red Sox cap and a T-shirt under his apron. A short-order cook was like one of those dancers on public television. Dad would be back there for eight hours on the rubber floor mats twirling and dipping. "It's all about the timing," he'd say. "Crack the eggs, drop the toast, flip the pancakes." Like ballet. I smiled at the thought of Dad in a tutu buttering a burger bun.

"Nell, food's up."

He slapped three plates on the ledge. Just for a

170

second our eyes met and he didn't smile or frown or anything. His face was red and shiny with sweat but he wasn't really there, just Ronnie, doing his job, his own self gone somewhere else.

He turned away and I took a quick breath. He was just so sad. The weight of it could drill a hole into the earth and suck everything down with it: the Far Reach, Fannie, George, Tom, Teddy and his crayons, all the old men sitting on their twirly stools, and me.

"Pick up, Nell," he called from back in the kitchen.

I slid out of the booth.

"Come on, Tom," I said.

We were quiet eating our pancakes. Fannie was too busy with customers to come over and pester us. Tom finished first. I don't think he ever chewed—just filled his mouth up and swallowed. "Slow down," Mom had said. "I've got no interest in swinging you from your ankles if you start choking." Tom had laughed.

Was it just me who cringed at the meanness? Just me who wondered if Mom would have bothered saving any of us if we were choking on our pancakes?

George came slamming through the swinging door to the kitchen carrying a plastic bin for dirty dishes.

"Hey, kids," he called over to us.

"Hi, George," said Teddy.

"Hey," said Tom.

I ignored him. *Kids?* Since when was he not a kid, too? He switched the empty bin for a full one, nodded at us, and went back into the kitchen, acting like everything was normal. I scrubbed my fork around in the syrup on my plate. I had more than half the money we needed for the trip. We could probably make another fifty with car washes and grocery bag tips. George should make up the difference. He should give Mt. Rushmore back and get his butt in the car when we were ready to hit the highway.

"Gonna head over to Carlos's house," said Tom. "We're going back to the Stop & Shop."

"Great," I said.

Teddy was the slowest eater on the planet. He took a bite, chewed it forever, took another, chewed and chewed. He stopped for a while, rearranged the food on his plate so it was centered, and took another bite. I got out #9. I only had a couple of chapters left.

After a while the morning rush slowed down and Fannie came over and slid herself onto the bench seat opposite Teddy and me.

"How're you holdin' up, sugar?"

"I'm okay."

She raised an eyebrow.

It would have been good to talk to Fannie about my fight with Maya, Mt. Rushmore, Mom, George, and everything. But she'd go straight to Dad with all of it. She couldn't help herself, thinking it would make things better. She'd told him about my period and now I was all alone in my bedroom. Talking to Fannie was sure to backfire.

Teddy finished his last bite of pancakes and set his fork down. Fannie smiled at him.

"I like your sunflower pin, honey pie. Where'd you get it?"

I froze. Teddy turned to me and I shot him a look.

"What's up, you two?"

"Nothing," I said.

"Nothing," said Teddy.

"Nothing, huh?" She raised her left eyebrow and stared hard at Teddy, trying to get him to spill the beans.

"Hey," yelled a guy at the counter. "Has the chicken laid my eggs yet?"

"Keep your shirt on," yelled Fannie. I'm not sure how she did it but her yelling was always friendly. She slid herself out of the booth. "Behave now," she said, looking straight at me.

"You bet," I said.

Behave? I figured selling all Mom's stuff at a yard sale qualified as serious misbehavior but I didn't care. President Nixon and me were both crooks. And that was just too bad.

Chapter 23

When we got home I sat at the kitchen table staring at the newspaper. The fan on the counter swung back and forth pushing the muggy air around. I wiped the sweat off my face with a paper napkin. Teddy and Abe were in the living room and Scooby-Doo was making a racket on the TV.

I turned to the horoscopes first. Mine made me nervous. What else could go wrong?

Taurus: Some unprecedented moves or unusual situations likely. Study all carefully so that you can cope effectively.

Mom's horoscope said she ought to *avoid any new investments or business partners.* That was one she'd hate since it was so off the wall. "Blow it out your ear," she'd say. "What am I? A bigwig on Wall Street?"

There was a special section in the paper about all the crimes Nixon was mixed up in—break-ins, burglary, bribery, cheating on his taxes, trying to cover it all up. A bunch of his aides had gone to jail. The paper was wrinkled and had coffee stains on it so I knew Dad had seen it. Was he starting to wonder about Nixon? At least the Red Sox were back in first place. That might balance things out a little for him but not for long. The Sox were bound to mess up their lead like they always did.

I knew from looking through Dad's books that the presidents on Mt. Rushmore weren't all that perfect, either. George Washington had won the Revolution but he owned slaves and so did Thomas Jefferson. They were two of the Founding Fathers of the whole country and they should have gotten rid of slavery right off the bat but they didn't.

Teddy Roosevelt set up lots of national parks but he shot animals for fun—wagonloads of beautiful wild animals. I'd seen pictures of the mountain goats and buffalo he shot. Dad had read all those books about his presidents but he never talked about the not-so-great stuff.

He didn't talk much about fighting the communists in the war in Korea, either. "I kept a postcard of Mt. Rushmore in my ditty bag over there. It was my good-luck charm," he'd said. When they showed soldiers in Vietnam on the news he was real quiet. Those soldiers were fighting the communists, too. Lots of people were dying every day on both sides. I'd seen the antiwar demonstrations in Cambridge on the Commons and on TV. Dad said they were traitors. I didn't think so. Not anymore.

Fighting in a war was something a person never got over. Tito Mendez, who lived two houses down, had always been a joker. When I was little he'd turn the hose on Maya and me as we walked by or set off a firecracker and scare us so bad we'd scream at the top of our lungs and he'd laugh his head off.

We were never really mad at Tito because we knew he wasn't trying to scare us in a bad way, just in an exciting way.

He was only twenty years old when he came back from Vietnam last year and he wasn't a joker anymore. He hardly ever left his house except to go to work at the Esso gas station on Highland Avenue where he was mostly alone under the hood of a car. Mrs. Mendez, his mom, was wrecked now, too. She hardly ever smiled.

And Stefan died.

Dad's Mt. Rushmore postcard hadn't been a very lucky good-luck charm. Maybe part of his deep-down sadness was from years and years ago when he was in

Korea seeing people getting killed like Tito had. A chunk of him was always going to be sad.

I reached into my pocket, pulled out my hopscotch stone, and rubbed the smooth surface with my thumb, hoping it was luckier than Dad's postcard. I wanted to call Maya. Get away from the newspaper and the Mt. Rushmore salt-and-pepper shakers sitting on the table, staring at me.

Tom and Carlos came tearing through the back door and I shoved the stone into my pocket.

"Hey," said Carlos.

"Here's more money." Tom dumped a pile of change on the table. "Two dollars and forty-five cents."

They got glasses of Kool-Aid and headed down to the basement. Tom and Carlos did everything together and liked the same stuff: G.I. Joes, model airplanes, baseball, and they shared a paper route. Mom said they were linked in some deep way. "Like long-lost twins."

I picked up Abe's water bowl and filled it at the sink. Even with the fan on the counter swishing back and forth it was hot and sticky in the kitchen.

I always thought Maya and me were linked in a special way, too. We always sat on the bus together, liked the same things: orange Popsicles, hopscotch, riding the subway, hot dogs not hamburgers.

When I turned eight, Mom said I was old enough to walk to Maya's by myself without getting lost or run over. Before that she made George go with me. I think he liked doing it—him being in charge, being the boss. He always held my hand crossing the street. I adored George back then and I think he liked me, too, although he wouldn't ever let me hug him.

When Teddy and Dad went to bed at eight o'clock I got up from the sofa and went into the kitchen. It was a mess—dishes from lunch and dinner piled up in the sink, food left out on the counter. Why was it me who always cleaned up? Made dinner? Because I was a girl. The only reason Tom was in the living room watching *Hawaii Five-O* was because he was a boy. Mom had ducked out on cleaning and cooking and kid watching and I got stuck with it because I was the girl. It wasn't right. Maybe I *was* a women's liberation girl and maybe I wasn't going to behave anymore.

I marched into the living room.

"Hey," I said. "Help me clean up."

Tom stared at me a second. "What?"

"You heard me. Help me clean up."

He followed me into the kitchen and stood there looking around. Tom didn't even know *how* to help. I handed him the broom and started on the dishes. But he just swept everything around in a muddle.

"Start on one side of the room and work your way across," I said.

I stood at the sink washing a saucepan, grinning like I'd won an Olympic medal or something. And it hadn't been that hard.

After we finished Tom settled on the couch to watch a western. I went upstairs and peeked into Teddy's room. He was asleep with *Mike Mulligan and His Steam Shovel* poking out from underneath his pillow. Abe was curled up on the blanket.

I walked back to my room, got into my pj's, and lay in bed wishing Abe had picked me to sleep with since I was the one who was all alone. It was just my luck he was a boy dog so of course he'd decided to sleep in the boys' room.

I bet more people had dogs than didn't have dogs. All the presidents had dogs, even Nixon. On TV he didn't look like someone a dog would warm up to but maybe the news cameras didn't pick up everything about a person.

My family was weird not to have had a pet until now. Maya had a cat, Louisa, who never went outside—a fat cat who looked like one of the pillows on the furniture. She was very old and never moved much, but purred when I stroked her back. Cats really did purr.

My family had a dog. There was someone who was happy living in our house, his tail wagging. Even though I liked Abe Lincoln the best of the four of them up on that mountain, I wasn't thrilled naming our dog after him. Abe Lincoln was a sad president. I could tell from the old-fashioned photos in Dad's books. His mom died when he was little and his son died while he was president. But he must have been funny sometimes. I'd read that he kept notes to himself in his top hat—that's pretty goofy. And then he got shot.

"Stop thinking about it," I whispered to myself. I had enough to worry about without feeling sad about poor Abe Lincoln. But I couldn't help it. I rolled over and punched at my pillow. I picked up #9 and finished the last chapter. Like always, Nancy Drew was brilliant and brave and everything was peachy in the end. But she didn't have a dog.

It was barely light out when Teddy banged open my door and woke me up. Abe came barreling in after him, jumped on my bed, and licked my face. I pushed him off and checked my alarm clock. It was six in the morning.

"What's going on?" I said.

"He has the itchies and now I've got 'em."

I reached over and turned on the light. Teddy was

scratching at his arm and Abe was sitting up on the end of my bed pawing at his ear.

"Let me see."

Teddy had bumps on his arms and neck like mosquito bites, but bigger and redder. Abe was full-out scratching now, all bent over, chewing at his belly.

"Off. OFF!" I pushed him onto the floor. "He's got fleas or something."

Bugs. I hated bugs. Especially bugs that bit. Our dog had brought us more than some happy. He'd carted in bugs. Jeesh.

Chapter 24

Teddy and Abe followed me downstairs. The kitchen light was on and Dad's work shoes were gone, which was a good thing considering the fleas. Tom's *Boston Herald American* bag was gone, too. He'd already left to do his paper route.

Outside, I checked the bungee cord on the front gate and we let Abe loose in the yard. Teddy sat on the front stoop and scratched at his itches. We had to do something about the fleas or Dad would have an excuse to get rid of our brand-new dog. I ran upstairs and got dressed.

Maybe the Morettis would know what to do. If they were awake. No one was on their porch but the lights were on downstairs. The minute I set foot on the front steps

Jack started barking like a crazy dog inside the house. Abe must have heard him because he started barking from our front yard, which made Jack bark even louder with a growl thrown in. In her bathrobe, Mrs. Moretti opened the front door but left the screen door closed to keep Jack inside.

"Is everything all right, Nellie?" she asked over the racket.

"What do I do about fleas?"

"Oh dear. Flea powder and a flea bath. You can pick up what you need at Walgreens. Treat the dog and pour some in the vacuum cleaner bag."

"In the bag?"

"You'll have to vacuum the whole house." She gave Jack a whack on his rump. "Quiet! The powder kills them in the bag. And if the dog's been on the beds, wash the sheets and blankets. Fleas are just terrible."

Back at the house I got Teddy a bowl of cereal and he ate outside, sitting on the stoop to keep Abe company. Walgreens in Porter Square didn't open until seven. I started a load of blankets in the washing machine, sat at the kitchen table, and ate my cereal while I started #10. Nancy got into serious trouble every five or six chapters—kidnapped, purse snatched, knocked out, car chased. It was hard to believe that her dad would let her do all the dangerous stuff she did. Her mom had died when she was three years old and they had a housekeeper, Mrs. Gruen, who loved Nancy but couldn't really tell her what to do since she wasn't her mother. Mrs. Gruen cooked, did the laundry, hemmed Nancy's dresses, and cleaned the house.

It would have been great to have had a friendly housekeeper show up after Mom left. But there wasn't much room in our house, and *my* Mrs. Gruen would have ended up sleeping in my room. Even though I was lonely in my bedroom, I didn't want to be roommates with some old lady.

We got to Walgreens right when the manager was unlocking the front door. Teddy stayed outside with Abe. I found the flea powder and flea shampoo in the pet aisle. Another three dollars of the Mt. Rushmore money gone.

"Tell your mom to put some of the flea powder in the vacuum cleaner bag. And she'll have to wash the bedding in hot water," said the cashier.

I wanted to tell the lady I already knew all that and also not everyone had a mom. I wasn't going to say anything at first, but she had this bossy voice and counted out my change really slowly like I was five years old or something.

"Ma'am, I don't have a mother. Neither did President Lincoln. You shouldn't assume everyone's got one and say stuff like that." My face got hot.

The lady put her hands together like she was praying. "I'm so sorry, dear."

I grabbed the paper bag and ran out of the store. It wasn't exactly fair to go after her, but too bad. I wasn't going to just let things go anymore. I wasn't going to behave.

It turned out that shampooing a dog wasn't easy. Abe didn't like getting wet and Teddy had to wrestle with him to hold him still while I soaked them both with the hose. I squirted a blob of shampoo on Abe's back.

"It says on the bottle not to get any in his eyes," I said. "And you shouldn't rub your eyes with the suds on your hands."

Teddy started scrubbing. Abe thought it was all a game. He got away from Teddy and wrapped the leash around my legs.

"Hold him still!"

Teddy just giggled while I untangled myself.

Abe stopped and shook, starting at his butt end all the way up to his floppy ears. Soapy water flew everywhere. I was soaked but I held tight to the leash while Teddy worked the soap down each leg and on Abe's chest and belly.

"That's good enough," I said.

I rinsed off Teddy first and then hosed down Abe. He liked that part, dancing around at the end of the leash.

"Go get your towel and we'll take him out front to dry off," I said.

Abe rolled around in the grass in the front yard and Teddy sat on the stoop in the sun, wrapped in his beach towel. I went inside and pulled the vacuum cleaner out of the hall closet, dumped some flea powder in a new bag and switched it with the old one.

Vacuuming the whole entire house was going to take forever. And I had to finish washing the sheets and blankets, too.

"Where's my Mrs. Gruen," I mumbled.

Tom came in the back door and hung his *Boston Herald American* bag on a peg. I hadn't even looked at the paper today.

"Why's the dog all wet?" he said.

"Fleas. We had to give him a flea bath."

"Does Dad know?"

"No. And we're fixing it."

He reached into his pocket and pulled out a square of tightly folded bills. "I got paid for my paper route. Here's fourteen dollars."

"Great."

"How much did you make on the yard sale?"

"A hundred and thirty-four dollars. Counting the fourteen we still need two hundred and twenty-eight bucks. Kind of a stretch."

"Do you think George'll come?" he said.

I shrugged.

"Doesn't matter." Tom kicked at the floor. "Not gonna happen anyway."

He turned before I could answer and went out the front door. His voice had been a giving-up voice. And he was right, too. There was no way we were going to fill that Maxwell House coffee can back up in two weeks. George had to help.

I left the vacuum cleaner in the living room and marched out to the front yard. The boys sat on the stoop while Abe lay on the grass chewing his rawhide bone.

"Tom, watch Teddy, will you."

"Where you going?" he asked.

"Far Reach. Be right back."

I yanked the bungee cord off the gate, slipped through, and hooked it shut again. My clothes were still wet from the flea bath but I didn't care. I walked fast, almost ran the whole way. The breakfast rush was over and Fannie was sitting at the counter with Dad drinking coffee.

They looked up when I came storming in.

"Gotta talk to George," I said, not stopping, breathing hard.

He was in the kitchen scrubbing a pot in the big stainless steel sink.

"Gotta talk to you," I said.

He turned and wiped his hands on his apron.

"What?"

"Out back."

"What's your problem?" he said.

I banged through the screen door into the alley behind the building. George followed me. I turned and glared at him.

"I've got two hundred and seventy-two dollars for the trip. You need to cough up the rest. And you've gotta come home."

"Forget it," he said, and turned to go back inside. I grabbed his arm.

"No, I'm not forgetting it. You shouldn't have stolen that money. We all need Mt. Rushmore, not just Dad. And we need you home."

"Why should I give a damn? He kicked me out."

Fannie opened the screen door and stuck her head outside.

"What's going on, kids?" she said.

"It's private," I said, giving her a go-away look.

"Okay, you're the boss." Fannie shut the screen door.

I turned to George. "You've got to come home."

"In your dreams."

"You did steal the money, you know. Just apologize to Dad."

"She needed it."

"George, please."

"Get off my back."

He turned and pulled open the screen door. I didn't grab his arm again. There was no point in saying another word to him. I'd been certain he'd understand. Certain that he'd see that Teddy and Tom needed this. That I did, too. That we all needed him to come home. To be a family. But he didn't care.

I kicked the side of the green dumpster sitting next to the screen door. The clunk echoed in the alley. I kicked it again. It didn't budge. And now my foot hurt and there were fleas in the house that I still had to vacuum up so Dad wouldn't haul Abe off to the dog pound.

I was steaming mad when I got home. Tom took off for Carlos's house and Teddy stayed in the yard with Abe. I went upstairs and stripped the sheets off my bed, yanking them hard, throwing them in a pile on the floor. I hauled the wet blankets out of the washer, shoved them in a laundry basket and started another load of sheets. After I'd hung the blankets on the line in the backyard I got to work vacuuming. I was a sweaty mess by the time I was done with the floors and couch and Dad's recliner. By the time I'd thrown the last load of sheets in the dryer I was ready to sit in Teddy's kiddie pool, read #10, and make the whole world disappear.

But it wasn't even lunchtime yet and I wasn't done. I brought the flea powder out to the front yard. Abe's coat was dry and at least he didn't stink anymore. I sprinkled the powder over his back and rubbed it in. He licked my face.

"All fixed," I said.

Teddy smiled and scratched at a flea bite on his neck.

"I'll get the calamine lotion," I said. "Then I'm gonna take a shower."

What I really wanted to do was go over to Maya's and sit outside with her on the bench at the bus stop in front of the store, drink a cold soda. Maya would get me laughing the way she'd go on about what a selfish pig George was and she'd probably spit, too. But I couldn't take a chance of finding Alien Maya when I got there. I was too close to crying, to busting apart. Heck, my family was already busted up. Mt. Rushmore was the glue that could put it back together and Tom was right—our big trip west wasn't gonna happen.

Chapter 25

Boston Herald American, July 22, 1974
Apollo 11 *Crew Gives Memento*
to Cathedral

After I finished getting rid of the fleas, Teddy and me had peanut-butter-and-jelly sandwiches for lunch. There wasn't much in the paper about President Nixon. But there was a story about the astronauts Neil Armstrong, Buzz Aldrin, and Michael Collins, who'd gone to the cathedral in Washington, DC, and donated a moon rock.

I was in second grade when they walked on the moon. We all watched. It was in the summer and the streets were empty. No cars moving, no people out walking their dogs. Everyone in the whole world watched. "Isn't that something," Dad had said. Even Mom sat on the couch with us glued to the TV.

My horoscope wasn't very hopeful.

Taurus: Mixed influences. You can hold your own through thoughtful management—plus a dash of imagination. Take possible setbacks in stride.

I couldn't see how my *imagination* was going to be any help at all today. And I didn't need any more *setbacks* after the flea invasion. Mom's horoscope made mine seem a million times worse.

Aries: Especially favored now: personal relationships, avocational interests, travel, and outdoor pursuits. A good day!

Setbacks for me and *a good day* for Mom. I was especially ticked off that she got an exclamation point. I needed one way more than she did.

Teddy was still eating.

"If you wanna visit the swan boats, finish your lunch."

"Okay."

He carried the bread bag and I had my school bag with #10 inside. When we got to our bench in the Boston Public Gardens, Crook flew in and landed at Teddy's feet. He handed her a crumb. I read for a while but it was hard to concentrate. I was getting tired of perfect Nancy Drew, her sports car, and all her adventures, and I kept thinking about Mom's exclamation point. She was off having *a good day!* while I was trying to fix Dad, who had no hope, and get George back home. Tom and

Carlos would have to lug a zillion grocery bags at the Stop & Shop and I'd have to pull a couple of square miles of weeds and wash a hundred cars to get us all to Mt. Rushmore.

I yelled over to Teddy.

"Come on. Gotta get home."

"There's still bread." Teddy reached into his bag and threw another handful out over the water. The ducks got into a scuffle, fighting over the crumbs.

I got up and started walking along the path to Charles Street. Teddy ran up behind me.

"Why're we leaving?"

"Because." He was wearing Mom's sunflower pin. Sunflowers were big, happy things. "Take that stupid pin off, Teddy."

He wrapped his small hand around it and looked at me like I'd stabbed him in the heart.

"Forget it," I said. "Sorry."

"Okay," he said, his eyes shiny.

When we crossed Charles Street I took his hand and gave it a squeeze. Like always, there was a group of hippies in tie-dye shirts and long hair sitting on the grass in the Commons. They had stuck two wobbly poles in the ground holding each end of a banner that said: IMPEACH NIXON NOW. A girl in the group called over to Teddy, "Hi, little man."

"Hi," he said.

It was the bright colors and laughter that pulled me over to them.

"Hi," said the girl. She was wearing a long, flowy skirt and dangly earrings. She patted on a patch of green grass and we sat down next to her.

"Hi," I said.

"Why are we sitting here?" asked Teddy.

"I don't know," I whispered.

"Why not?" said the girl, and she laughed.

If Dad saw me sitting under that IMPEACH NIXON NOW sign with a bunch of hippies, he'd probably kick me out of the house, too. But I didn't care because I had decided he was wrong. Nixon was a crooked president and he should get impeached.

"Why so sad?" asked the girl.

I didn't answer. She just smiled and waited. I wanted to tell her that my dad had had the money all saved up for our big road trip to Mt. Rushmore but my brother George stole it because my mom asked him to since she needed it for running-away money and Dad got in a fight with George and kicked him out of the house.

"My mom left. Ran away." That's all I said. But it was everything. And I'd said it to a complete stranger.

"That's awful." She took both my hands and held them.

I pulled away. Saying it out loud and someone hearing me say it got me real close to crying like that little kid with the pink pony all over again. Especially because remembering the pink pony reminded me that I was having a fight with Maya on top of everything else.

One of the guys in the group started playing his guitar. The girl got up and began to dance. Her long skirt, dangly earrings, and hair flew around as she twirled in circles on bare feet. The others laughed and clapped as the girl twirled and twirled.

Teddy got up on his knees and whispered in my ear, "Why's she dancing?"

"She must be happy." I put my arm around him.

"Oh."

Chapter 26

Dad was in his recliner reading the paper when we got back from the swan boats.

"Hi," I said.

"Hey, kids. Keep it down, would you," he said.

He didn't look at us, wanted silence. Wanted us to disappear.

"I'm taking Abe outside to pee," said Teddy. "And Mr. Solano's got the flag up."

"Check the gate before you go next door," I said.

I went out back, pulled the blankets off the line and carried them upstairs. I made my bed first and went into the boys' room. Tom was lying on his bed reading a Spider-Man comic book.

I sat down on Teddy's mattress. Tom flipped the page. Above him, three World War I fighter planes hung from hooks in the ceiling. Did he lie there at night watching them twirl in the breeze coming in the window? Did he imagine battles between the German and the British and American planes right above his head?

"Don't the planes keep you awake?" I asked.

Tom rolled over on his side and set his comic book down behind him on his bed. "No. If I stare at them long enough it puts me to sleep."

"Maybe I should borrow a couple."

"Sure."

George's bed was a tangled mess. It was just too sad to look at. I got up and pulled the sheets straight and tucked the blanket in.

"How long do you think he'll stay at Glenn's?" Tom asked.

"Who knows?"

"It's weird him not being here."

Tom stared at the planes twirling above him. The room was crammed with furniture, hot and messy with dirty clothes in heaps. I made up Teddy's bed, stepping over his wet bathing suit in the corner.

"I was counting on s'mores, too," said Tom, still looking up at his planes.

I jammed Teddy's pillow into the pillowcase. Tom hardly ever complained. Hardly ever caused problems. I forgot about him sometimes. He never started fights or blew his top—kind of invisible.

Back in March, the day Mom left, when we'd gotten off the school bus and walked into the house, Dad had said, "Your mother's gone. Suitcase is gone." Tom had slipped down to the basement and disappeared.

But now with George gone Tom couldn't slip away so easily, not with the empty bed right there in his room. Mom leaving had started up a bunch of bumper cars bashing into each other. Bad things just piling up. It's not like everything was perfect before but we were all together.

Abe barreled into the room and jumped up on Tom's bed.

"Hey, pup." He rolled Abe over and gave him a tummy rub.

"Fleas are gone," I said.

"He sure smells better."

He picked up his comic book and Abe settled in next to him.

After making Teddy's bed I went downstairs and out to the backyard. I wanted to call Maya. Ask her if she had any brilliant ideas on how to come up with two hundred and twenty-eight dollars. I'd have to try not to hang up if she started jabbering on about her date with stupid Joey. And why did I have to be the one who called? Maya should call *me*, knowing things were tough and we'd been best friends since kindergarten.

When I got back inside Dad was asleep in his chair and Teddy was coloring at the kitchen table. I got #10 and sat on the couch. I knew it was going to be another happy ending since Nancy had gotten nine happy endings already. I only wanted one and it was looking less and less likely.

I woke up in the dark. The phone in Dad's room was ringing and ringing. I turned on the light and blinked at the clock on my bedside table. The phone kept ringing. It was one o'clock in the morning. The ringing stopped. I heard Dad's muffled voice, his thumping footsteps, the toilet flush. He cracked my door open.

"Nell?"

"What's wrong?"

"That was a nurse at Boston City Hospital. George got in a fight."

"A fight?" I sat up. Dad didn't sound angry, just tired.

"I'll be back soon."

He thumped down the hall. I got up and went after him.

"Is he okay?"

He shut his bedroom door behind him. Didn't answer. Tom and Teddy and Abe came out in the hall. We all waited. Dad opened his door. He was dressed, tucking in his shirt.

"Go back to bed."

He passed us, thumped down the stairs, and the door slammed shut.

Abe and the boys followed me down to the kitchen. I poured three glasses of milk and grabbed the package of Oreos. We all sat at the kitchen table dunking cookies in the milk. Abe watched, his ears twitching like he knew there was something wrong. I got up and gave him a couple of dog biscuits. We sat there for a long time not talking, eating Oreos, drinking milk.

"He's gonna be a while," I said. "I'm going back to bed."

"Come on, Teddy," said Tom.

We all climbed the stairs. I left my door open so I'd hear George and Dad when they got home. Abe came in and jumped on my bed. I reached over and laid my hand on his back. His tail thumped against the covers. He seemed to know exactly who needed him the most at any moment of the day and he'd just show up.

I was never gonna fall asleep. George was hurt. In the hospital. Was Dad bringing him home? Who beat him up? Why? I dug my fingers into Abe's fur.

"Nellie."

Teddy stood in the doorway.

"Can't sleep?"

"Is George coming home?"

"Don't know."

He stood there. Waiting.

I got up and Abe jumped off my bed. I took Teddy's hand and we went into the boys' room. Teddy climbed into his bed, I got into George's bed and Abe hopped up with me. We all lay there in the dim light from the hallway.

"Do you think he's hurt bad?" asked Tom.

"Hope not."

We were quiet then. I could hear the boys breathing. I stroked Abe's back and he nestled closer. George's pillow stunk of the Old Spice aftershave he splashed all over his face every morning. He didn't have much more than a thin little mustache but he always shaved his whole entire face. Made a big show of it at first, taking forever, while everyone waited in the hall to use the bathroom.

I watched Tom's fighter planes spin. The silver parts glinted as they caught the light coming from the hall-way. After a while Teddy started kicking in his sleep. I smiled.

Chapter 27

Boston Herald American, July 23, 1974
*Lawyers Silent on Nixon Obeying
Supreme Court*

I got up really early. Dad's car wasn't in the driveway. Carlos showed up and he and Tom folded their newspapers and took off on their bikes. I sat at the kitchen table, half asleep, staring at the headlines. Lots of stuff about Nixon, subpoenas, the Supreme Court, and the secret tapes. I didn't give a darn about any of it. Dad should have called and let us know what was happening.

I flipped to my horoscope. That was a laugh.

Taurus: Keep plans flexible; changing situations could make revision necessary. On the personal side: romance and travel highly favored.

Yeah, sure. Today was going to be all about *romance.* Mom would have teased me like mad: "Nellie's gonna get a boyfriend today. Who's it gonna be, huh?" and she'd laugh her head off.

Her horoscope was absolutely correct. Especially the part that said: *Personal relationships under something of a cloud.* More like a hurricane since she'd blown up her *relationships* with everyone in her family.

I cracked open #10. Nancy was in her sports car chasing after a suspicious red truck when I heard Dad's Dodge Dart drive up and the engine turn off.

They came in together. Dad had his arm around George, helping him through the door. George's nose was bandaged up, and both his eyes were swollen almost shut. He had a busted lip, too, and his right hand had a bandage wrapped around it so I could only see the tips of his fingers poking out.

"We'll get you set up on the couch," Dad said.

George didn't say anything.

I held my breath. My brother was home but he was all broken.

Dad set a pillow on the end of the couch, pulled George's sneakers off and helped him stretch out. George groaned when he bumped his bandaged hand on the coffee table. Abe lay down alongside the couch.

"Hey, pooch. You're still here." George's voice was shaky and he mumbled a little with his split lip.

It was hard to look at his face. They'd put some small

bandages on his left eyebrow where he had a cut, and his eyes were puffy red slits. The huge white bandage taped on his nose made the swollen red parts look even worse.

"I've got to fill his prescription and get groceries," said Dad. "Keep an eye on him. The doctor said he's got bruised ribs and maybe a concussion."

George kind of rolled his eyes, at least what I could see of his eyes. Dad stood in the doorway for a minute, staring at him, shook his head, and left.

I sat in the recliner. It wasn't even seven o'clock yet so Dad would have to wait outside the store. Maybe he'd left because it was hard for him, too. To look at George's busted-up face.

"What happened?" I said.

"Couple of guys at a liquor store. Wouldn't buy me a lousy six-pack of beer. I guess they didn't like what I called them."

George was wheezing since he could only breathe through his mouth.

"How'd you end up at the hospital?"

"They said someone found me on the sidewalk. Out cold."

"Did they break your nose?"

"Yeah. Hurts like hell." He gently touched the bandage with his good hand.

"Wasn't Glenn with you?"

"No. I was over in Boston."

"Boston?"

His face went even more crooked.

"I took the bus from Boston out to Lowell. To see Mom. I knew the address. Mailed her the money. She's got an apartment now." His shoulders started to shake and he looked up at the ceiling.

"What happened?" I whispered.

"Asked her if I could live with her."

Tears rolled down from his swollen eyes and soaked into the bandage. He was crying. His whole busted-up body was crying.

"She said no, didn't she?"

"Wouldn't even let me in the door." George's words were broken up with his short wheezy breaths. "'It's gotta be a clean break or I can't do this,' she said."

I was quiet. Abe stood and put his head on the edge of the couch. George laid his bandaged hand on his back.

"I was on *her* side," he said.

He kind of laughed. I understood. Laughing was real close to crying sometimes. George was breathing a little easier now. I got up and wet a dish towel in cold water in the kitchen.

"Here," I said.

"Thanks."

He held the cool towel against his forehead. The

breeze coming in the window rattled the blinds. The sky was dark. I was glad. Rain would cool everything down.

"When I got back to Boston I was looking for a fight," George said. "Those guys were already drunk and bigger than me. Thought I could take 'em."

"Yeah," I said. "Guess you thought wrong."

He laughed again and grabbed his side with his good hand. "God, it hurts."

Tom came in through the back door and stared at George. At the same time, Teddy came downstairs in his pj's.

"Holy crap," said Tom.

George gave them a lopsided grin.

"I'm okay, guys," he said. And his voice was gentle in a big-brother way.

Tom and Teddy got their cereal and sat on the rug in the living room across from George to eat it. It was hard to tell if he was sleeping, with his eyes all swollen and mostly shut.

"You awake?" I whispered, and he nodded.

Dad got back from the store and Tom helped him with the grocery bags.

"Here's your painkiller," Dad said. "How're your ribs?"

George struggled to sit up.

"Hurts. Thanks."

I got out of Dad's recliner and he sat down with his newspaper. In the kitchen I put the groceries away. Teddy tried to help but he was too short to reach the cupboards.

"Take Abe out to pee," I said.

Tom came in and opened the basement door.

"At least he's back," he said.

I could hear Dad snoring. He'd been up almost the whole night and he wasn't the best person to keep an eye on things. I went into the living room and touched George's shoulder. He shook my hand off. "Just let me sleep, would you," he said in his grumpy George voice.

I sat on the rug, opened my book, and looked over at my brother. The getting-beaten-to-a-pulp part was awful but the getting-him-back part was good.

Chapter 28

It rained all morning. George dozed on and off with Abe curled up by his feet on the couch. Teddy watched cartoons with the sound on low while Dad snored in his recliner. He was asleep most of the morning.

With his bruised ribs George hobbled around like Mr. Solano on his bad hip. Tom helped him upstairs to the bathroom a couple of times and I made bologna-and-cheese sandwiches for everyone for lunch.

When the rain stopped I sat on the front stoop and watched Teddy play with Abe in the yard, throwing one of Tom's old baseballs. Abe raced after the ball and grabbed it in his slobbery mouth but refused to give it back unless Teddy gave him a dog biscuit.

Back inside I sat at the kitchen table in front of the

fan with #10. Nancy Drew had two friends who treated her like a queen. Bess was a scaredy cat, and George, who was a girl, was brave and athletic but not braver or more athletic than Nancy. They weren't real friends since they didn't get into fights and they never talked to each other about anything important. And perfect Nancy was always the boss.

Dad had lost hold of his friends since Mom left. A couple of nights a week he used to go to Benny's Tavern and hang out with his buddies in the neighborhood for an hour. "Off he goes to sit on his bar stool—the life of the party," Mom would say. He hadn't been there in months and his friends never came by to sit on the stoop and have a beer like they used to. Dad didn't work at keeping hold of them even though they'd known each other since they were kids.

Summer noises drifted in through the open windows—kids yelling, music, lawn mowers, people laughing in backyards. Maya should have called me. The longer I waited for the phone to ring the worse it was going to get, like a crack in the sidewalk that filled with dirt and weeds and got wider and wider.

I slammed #10 down on the table, got the phone, and dialed.

Mrs. Machado answered. I almost hung up.

"Maya there?"

"She's off with Marta, shopping. How are you, Nellie?"

"Fine."

"Marta has to go to work at five so they'll be back in a few hours."

"Okay. Thanks."

I wasn't going to try again. It was too hard. Everything was too hard. And it had turned out to be the worst kind of muggy day after all the rain. George's face was going from red to black to blue. And Mom was in her apartment all to herself with a *cloud over her relationships*, making a clean break. It wasn't clean. It was a dirty, lousy, crappy break. George had trusted her. And now look at him.

"Go to hell, Mom," I whispered.

I grabbed the bread bag and stuffed it with the last of the stale bread from the Far Reach.

Dad was asleep in his chair. Teddy was lying on the floor coloring next to George, who was asleep on the couch. I held up the bread bag. Teddy nodded. Abe lifted his head off George's foot.

"Stay, boy," whispered Teddy.

* * *

The Boston Commons was almost empty with dark clouds hanging low over our heads but the Impeach Nixon Now group of hippies was in their spot. The dancing girl waved and came over to us. Her clothes and long hair were wet from the rain but she didn't seem to care.

"Hi again, little man," she said to Teddy. "Where you going?"

"To feed the birds," he said, holding up the bread bag.

She looked at me and smiled. "Can I come?"

When we got to our bench I brushed most of the water off and sat down. The girl and Teddy fed the pigeons and he introduced her to Crook. He went over to the edge of the lagoon to feed his ducks and the girl sat next to me on the bench.

"Your little brother's cool," she said.

"Yeah, he is."

"I'm going to visit my brother in California in a couple of weeks. They have pelicans out there. Your brother would love them."

"California. Wow. We were going on a road trip to South Dakota. But it's not happening anymore."

"South Dakota?"

"To see Mt. Rushmore."

She was quiet, ran her fingers through her damp hair.

"My dad," I said. "He's got a thing about it. And the four presidents up there."

"It's a sacred mountain, you know," she said. "The government stole it from the American Indians."

"Sacred?"

"For the Lakota Sioux tribe it's a holy place. Carving that mountain up was a horrible thing to do."

"I didn't know."

"You should go see the Grand Canyon. They haven't messed that up too much," she said.

The girl went over to watch Teddy feed his ducks. My butt was wet from the bench. The ducks were squabbling over a hamburger bun and the girl and Teddy were laughing.

I kicked at the gravel at my feet. Mt. Rushmore was never complicated. The presidents up there weren't perfect but the mountain was always just a mountain. Now it turns out it was a sacred place for American Indians and those faces wrecked it, like graffiti on a church, or worse since it can never be undone.

Ever since I was a little kid I believed that mountain was a magical place. But it was really a messed-up place—a stolen mountain with presidents carved into it who didn't come close to being like the paintings of the saints with golden halos over their heads on the walls at St. Norbert's Catholic Church.

My rotten mom had stolen Mt. Rushmore. And before I was even born the government had stolen it, too. And I was doing everything I could to drag my falling-apart family out west to see it. Nothing made sense anymore.

Teddy and the girl came and sat on the bench next to me.

"I was named after Susan B. Anthony," I said. "A group of women back in 1938 wanted her face up on Mt. Rushmore, too."

"Didn't know that," said the girl, smoothing out her long skirt over her knees.

"I'm glad she's not up there now," I said.

"I'm glad, too." She nodded. She knew what I meant. "Hey, I've got to get back to my friends. That was fun, little man."

We waved goodbye and the girl smiled at me. A wide-open smile that wasn't complicated at all.

I put my arm around Teddy. "Hey, wanna go for a swan-boat ride?"

He jumped up from the bench. "Sure!"

There was no line at the dock. I bought our tickets and we got right on the boat. Teddy picked the front bench and I sat next to him. The swan boat moved slowly around the lagoon and the ducks paddled after us hoping for more bread.

Thirteen years old was much older than twelve, I decided. What with boobs and periods and not seeing Nixon or those presidents up on that stolen mountain as perfect anymore I was tired out. The swan-boat ride was nice and slow and the water wasn't deep. I didn't want it to end.

Chapter 29

Boston Herald American, July 24, 1974
President Must Surrender Tapes,
Supreme Court Rules: 8–0

Wednesday morning Dad got George downstairs and back on the couch. The headline was in huge black letters. The Supreme Court didn't buy any of Nixon's arguments. He had to obey the subpoena and hand over the tape recordings. Dad shook his head. "He's a goner. The Republicans are gonna turn on him now." But he didn't seem too upset with the news, which surprised me. I guess even Dad was starting to wonder.

As usual, my horoscope was way off.

Taurus: An excellent day in which to formulate long-range plans. Something which has seemed out of reach is closer than you may imagine.

My *long-range plans* for a trip to Mt. Rushmore weren't any closer than they were yesterday. Mom wasn't going to like hers much, either—*Your judgment still somewhat off.* Her judgment was off when she walked out the door. Nothing had changed.

"Laundry day, Nell," said Dad.

It was the way he said it. Not mean or anything but a friendly reminder. He had no clue that it wasn't fair. But I was done being singled out for dishes and laundry and sweeping up everyone's messes just because I was the only girl left in the house.

George had a good excuse with his bruised ribs. It was Dad's day off. But Tom and Teddy were just lying there on the living room floor watching TV.

"Hey, you two," I said. "Bring all the dirty clothes downstairs."

"Since when?" said Tom.

"Since now." I walked over and shut off the TV. "I'm not your housekeeper."

George gave me a lopsided stare. Dad looked over at my brothers and shrugged his shoulders.

"Help your sister, boys," he said.

Maybe Dad didn't know any better and just needed me to set him straight. I didn't know why he took my side but he did.

The boys made a racket throwing all the clothes down the stairs with Abe chasing after them, while I got a load of greasy Far Reach work clothes going in the washing machine.

"Make two piles," I said. "Light colors and dark colors."

"Okay," said Teddy.

Abe climbed on top of the mountain of dirty laundry and settled in for a nap.

"Off!" Teddy tried to lift Abe's rear end to move him.

"Likes the stink," said Tom.

Dad got out of his recliner. "Time to wash the car."

He pulled on his Red Sox cap and went out the back door to shine up his Dodge Dart like he used to every Wednesday. Even though George groaned if he moved the wrong way, and his face was a mess, we were all having a pretty good day—almost like a regular family. Maybe my horoscope was right. Being a regular family had seemed *out of reach* and here it was right in front of me.

I was pulling the wet work clothes out of the washer and shoving them in the dryer when I heard her voice. Mom's voice.

I ran out the front door with Teddy and Tom behind me. We stood on the stoop. Didn't get any closer. She was halfway to the house, inside the gate. Her hair was longer, almost to her shoulders. Dad was on the other side of the

218

chain-link fence in the driveway holding the hose, the water running out, forming a puddle around his bare feet.

"You've got a lot of nerve showing up back here."

"I just want my things, Ron."

"So where'd you get the car?"

"Borrowed it."

Mrs. Longmire stormed across the street, her pink housedress in a tangle. "That daughter of yours sold your clothes and books. Even your jewelry. Had it all laid out on the street with strangers walking off with everything. That foreign girl was egging her on."

Dad turned and stared at me. "You what?"

"You sold my things?" yelled Mom.

"I had a yard sale." There. I said it straight out. They could all just lump it.

Teddy climbed down the stairs and ran up to Mom. He didn't try to hug her, just stood there a foot away, his head tipped up, smiling. She ignored him, dug around in the pocket of her skirt.

Mrs. Longmire had a satisfied look on her face like she'd stirred up a hornets' nest and was plenty happy about it. "I tried to stop her. Got a lot of lip for my trouble."

"Get the hell out of here, Longmire," Dad yelled. "Now."

She backed away. "Well, I never! I can see why you left him, Connie."

"Get lost, Tina," said Mom, lighting up a cigarette.

Mrs. Longmire huffed some but turned around and walked back across the street to her house.

Teddy was still standing there, waiting. I studied my mom, the coldness of her, and I was glad I'd sold all her stuff.

"Just leave," I said.

Mom took a drag on her cigarette and looked over at Dad. "Little Nellie's found herself a spine, hasn't she?"

"Leave her alone," he said.

Mom turned and walked to a beat-up station wagon parked on the street. She got inside, slammed the door, and started the engine.

Teddy ran after her and Abe came charging out the front door, through the open gate, after him.

"Watch it!" yelled Dad.

"Stop!" I yelled.

But she didn't. Mom backed up to pull out of the parking space. When the car hit Abe he screamed a horrible dog scream.

We all ran toward the street.

The station wagon's brakes screeched. Mom got out.

"Oh God," she said.

I stared down at Abe, lying alongside the curb. He whimpered, tried to get up. I knelt down. His back leg was bloody and bent all wrong for a dog's leg. His eyes were wild as I stroked his back.

"It's okay, little guy."

Tom and I lifted him up out of the street, careful not to let his hurt leg move. He panted, his tongue hanging out, as we set him on the grass by the sidewalk.

Mom crouched down and touched Abe's heaving side. "I'm sorry. I didn't see him."

I turned. Mom was crying, a quiet crying with a face I'd never seen, sad and alone. She sank down on the grass next to me and Abe and Tom, put her hand on my shoulder. "I'm so sorry. About everything. I just couldn't. Couldn't do it. Day after day. I never wanted any of this." She swung her arm, taking in the house, Tom, me, Dad.

"But you just disappeared," I said, tears dripping down my face.

"I had to. If I saw you, any of you, I couldn't stay away."

"So come back. Just come back." My nose was running and I was crying full out. Tom was crying, too. Dad stood on the sidewalk, his face tight.

Mom shook her head. She reached over and put her arms around me, pulled Tom over and held us both tight. Then she let go. She let go of us and pushed on the ground with her hand spread wide. She stood, straightened her shoulders, and wiped at her eyes. "I'm sorry."

I watched as Mom got back in her car and drove away.

Dad gazed up the empty road, turned, and walked back toward the house.

Tom wiped his face with his T-shirt and got up on his knees next to Abe, who was quiet now but breathing hard. "Is he okay?"

"No," I said. "His leg's busted."

I looked back at the house. Dad was sitting on the stoop, his head in his hands. George stood in the doorway, the bandage on his nose bright white against the black bruises.

"Dad, we've got to get him to the vet!" I yelled.

He looked at me, shaking his head. "I would if I could. But we're flat broke."

"What do you mean? His leg's broken. He's bleeding."

"Had to pay the hospital and docs and medicine for George, and things were already tight."

"But he's hurt bad," said Tom, crying again, stroking Abe's head.

It was Tom sitting there alone that made me snap my head up and scan the street, the front yard.

"Where's Teddy?"

I got up and ran past Dad into the house.

"Teddy?" I yelled. "George, have you seen him?"

"He went upstairs for a minute, then out the back door."

I ran outside and around the back.

Teddy was gone.

Chapter 30

I raced up the stairs, yanked open my closet door, and pulled the sock with the Mt. Rushmore money out of the pocket of my winter coat. Taking two steps at a time I tore down the stairs and out the front door. George was standing by the car. Tom and Dad were crouched down by the curb moving Abe onto a towel.

"I can't find Teddy," I yelled.

"Jesus, what next?" Dad stood up, looked around like Teddy would just magically show up. "He's probably hiding under a bed or something."

"Here," I said, shoving the heavy sock into his hand.

"What's this?"

"Money. For the vet. It was for Mt. Rushmore but there's not enough."

"My God," said Dad, shaking his head. "You kids are something."

Abe whimpered—one little cry.

"We've got to fix him," said Tom.

"We're going to." Dad handed me back the sock. "George just gave me a hundred bucks for the vet."

I turned and stared at George, all battered up, the biggest cheapskate of all time. He shrugged.

"Let's get him in the car," said Tom.

"Got to find Teddy first," said Dad. "Stay with him so he doesn't try to stand on that leg. We won't be long."

George and Dad and I searched the house—every closet, under every bed, down in the basement. He wasn't anywhere.

"Dog will have to wait." Dad grabbed his wallet and his car keys out of the bowl on the kitchen counter. "I'm going to drive around. Cover more ground that way." His voice sounded worried. Teddy was really missing. "George, call Glenn and see if he can drive you and the dog to the vet." He pulled a wad of bills out of his pocket and set it on the table. "Here's the money you gave me. And here's the vet's address over by Inman Square." He set a page torn out of the phone book next to the cash.

George held on to his side with the bruised ribs with one hand and grabbed the phone in the other.

225

Dad turned and gave me a serious look. "You keep searching the neighborhood. Tell Tom to stick with the dog until Glenn gets here. And he should stay by the phone in case someone's found Teddy and tries to call."

He turned and ran out the back door to his car. All of Dad's rushing and giving orders got me even more scared. Teddy was missing. Really missing.

George hung up the phone. "Glenn's on his way."

When he tried to lean down to get his shoes by the door he stopped halfway, groaned, and squeezed his eyes shut. He'd already been climbing the stairs and looking under beds for Teddy when he was supposed to be on the couch.

"Sit down," I said, and picked up his sneakers.

George didn't argue, so it must have hurt something fierce. I pulled his sneakers on his feet and tied up the laces.

"Thanks," he said.

"You should lie down till he gets here."

"I'm okay."

But he did hobble over to the couch and he did lie down, breathing hard. I got a bowl of water and carried it outside. Tom was sitting in the driveway, Abe's head in his lap.

"How is he?"

"Can't tell. He's not panting much anymore."

Abe was so still. He ignored the water, just lay there with his eyes open. I sat on the pavement with Tom. Could a broken leg kill a dog? He was still bleeding and there was gravel mashed up in the cuts on his leg.

Glenn honked his horn and drove partway into the driveway. George limped outside while me and Tom carried Abe on the towel and laid him on the back seat of Glenn's Chevy. Abe didn't fuss, didn't whimper. George got in the back seat on the other side, scooted over, and rested his arm on Abe's back.

Glenn, a big kid with a round head and a crew cut, turned around and stared down at Abe. "You sure he's not dead already?"

"No, doofus," said George. "Head over to Inman Square."

Tom and I watched as Glenn backed out of the driveway.

"I'm going to search close by," I said. "Stay by the phone in case someone finds him and calls."

I walked around the neighborhood, asking people on the street if they'd seen a six-year-old boy wandering around alone. Two streets over, John and Eddie almost ran me down on their skateboards.

"Hey, wait a second," I yelled after them.

They stopped, flipped their boards up, and turned.

"What's going on?" said John.

"We can't find Teddy. Can you guys help search? He's got a blue T-shirt on and shorts."

"Sure," said John.

They got back on their boards and zipped down the sidewalk.

"If you find him bring him home," I yelled.

Eddie raised his hand and gave a thumbs-up.

The Haberman twins agreed to look but they weren't allowed to go far. No one else was around.

When I got to the house I noticed that Mr. Solano's flag was up. I raced around to the back, climbed up on the bench along the fence, and peered into his yard, expecting to see Teddy crawling around under the bushes, hunting down tennis balls. He wasn't. Mr. Solano was on his porch filling a bird feeder.

"Have you seen Teddy?"

"Nope. Been expecting him."

"We can't find him."

"Probably took that new dog of yours for a walk."

I didn't answer him. I couldn't think about Abe right then. When I got back inside Tom was sitting at the kitchen table staring at the phone.

"No calls?" I said.

He shook his head. And right then the phone rang. We both laughed. A quick, wasn't-that-weird laugh. I answered it.

"It's me," said George. "Did Teddy show up?"

"No. How's Abe?"

"Broken leg and some stitches. We'll be here a couple of hours. He's okay."

A-okay, I thought and took a sharp breath.

"Bye." I turned to Tom. "Abe's gonna be fine."

He got up. "I'll be right back. Gonna get Carlos."

I picked up the phone and dialed.

Maya answered.

"Teddy's run away," I said, almost yelling.

"What?"

"And my mom came and now she's gone." I wanted to cry. Because of everything that had happened and because Maya was there, on the phone, and I was talking to her.

"I've got to find Teddy."

"I'm coming," she said, and hung up.

I grabbed a kitchen towel, sat down at the table, and scrubbed at my face. Where was he? Where would he go? I couldn't just sit there. I threw the dish towel onto the counter and ran upstairs and into the boys' room. *Mike Mulligan and His Steam Shovel* wasn't on Teddy's bed or under his pillow or on the floor. He'd taken it with him.

"Nellie!" called Maya.

I ran downstairs.

"I know where he went!" I grabbed the sock off the kitchen table and pulled out a couple of bucks. "C'mon."

"Wait. Where?" said Maya.

"The swan boats."

"Would they let him on the subway?"

"I don't know. But he knows how to get there."

I checked the pegs by the washing machine. The bread bag was hanging there. But there wasn't any bread left. I knew it was stupid but I was sure if I brought bread for his birds Teddy would have to be there. I grabbed the bag and a new loaf of bread off the counter and handed them to Maya.

Carlos and Tom came racing into the kitchen.

"We're going to the swan boats," I said. "He might be there."

"Boston?"

"Stay by the phone."

We ran all the way to Porter Square. We didn't even take the long way to avoid Maya's street. Standing on the platform I tried to catch my breath.

"She ran over our dog," I said.

"Your mom?" said Maya, breathing hard.

"Yeah. She came to get her stuff and it was awful."

Maya whistled. I grabbed her arm. "I missed you."

"Me too," she said. "And Joey *is* stupid. Tried to put his hand up my shirt. I told him no and he didn't listen."

I stared at her. "What did you do?"

"Punched him."

"Hard?"

"Yeah, right in the stomach."

The train roared into the station stirring up the dust and litter on the platform. I started giggling and Maya laughed. The doors to the train *whoosh*ed open and we got on. When we sat down I held tight to the bread bag.

"We'll find him," said Maya.

"Do you think he got through the turnstile? Wouldn't the lady in the booth tell him to go home?"

"He's pretty short. Maybe he snuck through."

We sat, shoulders touching, as the train climbed out of the tunnel, crossed the bridge over the Charles River, and headed down into the dark once more.

Again we ran. Through the Commons, across Charles Street, and down the paved path toward the lagoon. And there he was, sitting on our bench, feet not even touching the ground, his book open in his lap.

"Teddy!"

He didn't smile when he saw us. He didn't close his book, either.

Out of breath, we sat on either side of him. He stared down at the last page of the story with the drawing of Mike and Mary Anne, the steam shovel, in the basement.

"What're you doing here?" I said.

He looked up at me, not crying, his face pinched. "Is Abe dead?"

"No. He's at the doctor's. They're fixing his leg."

A swan boat drifted by and Teddy watched it carefully.

"Why'd you come all the way here?"

"To see Mom." He reached up and gripped his sunflower pin.

"What?"

"Abe was hurt. She left and this is where she comes when she's sad. She said so. I knew she'd come. To see me. Because she forgot to say hello."

"Teddy. She wants to forget. That's what she's like."

He stared down at the last page in his book. At the happy ending in the cozy basement. I put my arm around him.

"We brought some bread." Maya held up the bag. "You gonna feed your birds?"

He shook his head, held tight to his book. The three of us stared out at another swan boat gliding under the footbridge. A pigeon circled over the water, turned, and flew toward us. It landed on the path in front of our bench.

It was Crook.

Teddy took the bread bag from Maya and handed *Mike Mulligan and His Steam Shovel* to me for safekeeping.

Chapter 31

found a pay phone outside Park Street Station. Tom answered on the first ring.

"I've got him," I said.

"He okay?"

"Yeah. Made it all the way to the swan boats by himself."

The train back was almost empty. The three of us sat on the long bench seat.

"How'd you get past the lady in the booth?" asked Maya.

"There was a family," Teddy said. "I pretended."

"What do you mean?" I asked.

"I pretended it was my family and stayed close."

Maya whistled. "Smart cookie."

Teddy wasn't staring out the window searching for rats like he always did. The way he sat holding tight to his book and the empty bread bag, his skinny legs not reaching the floor, he looked so small. I put my arm around him.

Whenever we went to see the swan boats Teddy had spent a lot of time checking out the paths and the footbridge. I always thought he was just curious about all the people. But he'd been searching for Mom, loving her all that time she was gone like he loved her before, with a smile on his face when she read him *Mike Mulligan and His Steam Shovel* or made some mean crack about him.

Mom was a lousy mother but the lousiest to Teddy because he still trusted her. George, too—he'd been on her side, stolen money for her, was sure of her, like Teddy. And she'd stomped all over their sureness, all over their hearts.

And she'd stomped all over Dad's heart, Tom's heart, and my heart, too. And when she was done stomping she left a second time.

I tightened my grip on Teddy and wiped at the tears on my face with my free hand. Maya put her arm around my shoulder and kept it there all the way to Porter Square.

On the walk home we stopped at the playground.

"Bring your throwing stone, tomorrow," I said to Maya.

"Still got it. In my makeup bag," she said. "Hey, I better get back or I'm so busted."

She knelt down and took hold of Teddy's shoulders. "See you, buddy. Gotta go dust the shelves in the store."

I watched regular Maya walk across the street like she owned it. Alien Maya was Maya, too, someone not afraid to use her fists on anyone who crossed the line. Both of them were my best friends, it just took some getting used to. And maybe I'd let her pierce my ears after all. I liked the look of those dangly earrings the dancing hippie girl wore.

George was on the couch when we got home. Tom was sitting on the floor with Abe, who was curled up on a blanket by the coffee table. His back leg was in a cast. When we saw him he tried to get up. Tom held him still.

Teddy ran over and sat on the floor on the other side of Abe, stroked his back, leaned in for a lick on his face. George gave Teddy a pat on the head.

"We looked all over for you, squirt."

Teddy smiled up at him.

"Dad's not back yet?" I asked.

"No. Called once but I didn't know you'd found him yet," said Tom.

Fannie showed up. She stormed through the front

door like the house was on fire and she had to save everyone.

"Teddy! You're safe." She plunked down on Dad's recliner, breathing hard. "Ron called. Said you ran off. Scared me half to death. Where were you?"

I filled her in and she gave Teddy the eye.

"Don't you ever do that again. Not ever. Hear me?"

He nodded and she held her arms out, waiting. He got up and walked over without any fuss. Fannie pulled him up on her lap and buried him in her arms. He soaked up that giant hug for a full minute, then pushed himself off and scrambled back down to the floor next to Abe.

"George, you look terrible," said Fannie. "How's the nose?"

"Doesn't hurt as much," he said.

"And how's the pooch?"

"Leg's broken," said Tom.

Fannie looked at me.

"How are you, honey?"

"I'm okay now," I said. "Thinking of getting my ears pierced."

"Oh my God, don't let your dad hear you say that."

"I don't care if he hears it or not. They're my ears."

George laughed. Fannie laughed, too, a belly laugh.

"Poor old Ronnie. Got his hands full with this crowd."

Fannie stayed awhile. Changed George's bandage on his nose while he complained the whole time. Teddy and Tom and Abe watched TV. After Fannie left I waited at the kitchen table for Dad.

When we heard the Dodge Dart pull into the driveway Tom ran outside.

"Teddy's here!" he yelled.

Dad ran inside and went straight for Teddy. He picked him up and held him in a bear hug. Teddy hugged him back, his head resting on Dad's chest.

"You scared the heck out of me."

"Sorry," said Teddy.

"No running off ever again."

"Okay."

Dad set Teddy down next to Abe and walked with me back into the kitchen. "Where was he?"

"At the swan boats waiting for Mom."

Dad shook his head. "Poor little guy."

"He wasn't one bit scared. Just really sad."

Dad picked up the sock full of money off the kitchen table. Stared at it for a while then set it down.

He walked over to me, took my hands, and pulled me up out of my chair. And he hugged me. A hug like when I was little. And I started crying because he was hugging me and Mom had really left and I could hardly breathe with the hiccupping tears pulling at my shoulders. And he started crying, too. And then I was crying worse than before and he sat down on one of the kitchen chairs and got me in his lap and wiped the tears off my face while his tears dripped down on his sweaty T-shirt.

"I'm sorry, Nell. It's been all on you."

"Yeah," I said. All of it had been on me—to keep my family from flying apart in every direction. "It has."

"And you're right about the laundry and all the rest," he said. "The boys have got to do their share around here."

I sat there in my dad's lap and laid my head on his shoulder. He smelled pretty bad from running around all day but I didn't mind. He wasn't perfect. There were probably going to be lots of times when he climbed into bed because the world was hard for him to be in. But right then I had him back, and George and Tom and Teddy and even Abe, too, who was going to be a-okay.

Chapter 32

Our campsite was tucked into a stand of pine trees, or at least that's what I thought they were. We'd pitched the three tents side by side, but by late afternoon the canvas was sagging in the middle, threatening to collapse.

"Need to teach you kids how to tie a half hitch," said Dad.

Teddy and me watched as he tightened all the ropes and tied them off in a series of complicated loops.

"That looks better," he said, standing by our campfire in jeans and a T-shirt.

"Is it time?" asked Teddy, sitting on a rock with Abe's head in his lap.

"Hot dogs first," said Dad.

Tom and George were off somewhere in the woods on a trail, probably getting lost. George just had a small bandage on his nose now and the bruises on his face had gone all green and yellow, but he was walking better.

The woods went on forever up the side of the mountain and it scared me a little, especially with the sun going down and the long shadows on the ground. Dad had set up a lantern on the picnic table and there were other campers nearby. But I was glad our Dodge Dart was right there, in our assigned spot, all ready for a quick getaway if a bear or a moose showed up.

Before we left, Teddy had gotten Carlos to promise he'd take care of Mr. Solano's tennis balls if the flag was up. Maya'd given me a box of Kotex just in case I got my period in the wilderness. I'd stashed it way in the bottom of my bag with my favorite hopscotch stone, which turned out to be pretty lucky after all.

New Hampshire was plenty far enough away from home. Dad wouldn't take the money I'd earned watching Teddy all summer and he wouldn't take any more from George.

"We should go someplace closer," I'd said.

"Now, there's an idea. How much did you make on that yard sale of yours?" he'd asked, smiling a little.

"Hundred and thirty-four dollars."

"That'll get us to New Hampshire and buy groceries for a week. Might even have enough left to pick up some Red Sox tickets, although the bums'll lose for sure."

I figured, fair is fair. Mom wasn't coming back.

Fannie came over to the house a couple of days before we left. We sat in the kitchen by the fan.

"Have you heard from her?" she asked.

"No. She didn't even call to see how Abe was doing after she ran over him. She's a lousy mom," I'd said.

"She's still your mom," said Fannie. "You'll forgive her in time."

"I don't have to forgive her. It's not a rule," I'd said. "It's up to me."

And it was up to me. It didn't matter what Fannie said or what my horoscope said. I got to decide if I was ever going to forgive my mom.

I'd given Maya back her thirty-seven dollars, and Tom his fourteen dollars and all the tip money he and Carlos had made at the Stop & Shop. His Huey Helicopter was hanging in the basement, and he'd bought a model kit for an Indy 500 race car. I was glad to see he was branching out, building a vehicle that stayed on the ground and out of wars.

I'd gone to Radio Shack with Maya and picked out

a record player with stereo speakers and I'd bought three albums already—the Beatles, Joni Mitchell, and Stevie Wonder. At first I was going to set it up in my room but decided I'd put it on the counter in the kitchen where it belonged. Dad wasn't thrilled but I turned the music down when he was around.

We'd made it to the campground in three hours. It cheered Dad up that we were in the White Mountains since a bunch of them were named after presidents. On August ninth, the day before we left for New Hampshire, Nixon resigned and his vice president, Gerald Ford, became the new president. After the secret tapes came out and proved Nixon was a crook, Dad was disgusted. "He was a disgrace to the office."

George and Tom got back from their hike and we all sat around the picnic table and ate hot dogs and baked beans. The food tasted pretty good, and it was nice and cool in the mountains.

"Is it time?" asked Teddy when we got back from a trip with flashlights to the bathroom down the path.

"It's time," said Dad.

We stuck marshmallows on sticks we'd collected that afternoon, and roasted them over the fire. The glow of the flames lit up everyone's faces in a bubble of light. Teddy's marshmallows lit on fire and he swung his stick

around like a sparkler on the Fourth of July while everyone laughed and Abe barked. I helped him squish his
burned marshmallows on a graham cracker and he stuck
half a Hershey's chocolate bar on it and finished it off
with another cracker.

He sat at the picnic table holding it carefully in both
hands.

"I've been thinking a lot about so mores," he said.

"Just eat it, squirt," said George.

And we all watched, even Abe, as Teddy took his
first bite, getting chocolate and melted marshmallow all
over his face.

"How is it?" I asked.

"Good," said Teddy. "Real good."

I put together my s'more and so did Tom, George,
and even Dad. There was no chance we'd run out of sup-
plies since Fannie had given us an entire case of Hershey's bars, five bags of marshmallows, and three boxes of
graham crackers for our trip. "Emergency rations," she'd
said, and winked.

"I'm gonna make another so more," said Teddy,
pushing a couple of marshmallows on his stick. We all
laughed and he grinned.

I'd never slept outside before. Dad had his own tent
and George and Tom were in another. Me and Teddy and

Abe were in ours. Abe was curled up between us as best he could with a cast on his back leg. I pulled my sleeping bag up to my chin in the cold night air.

"Are we really going to see Moocher and Minnie and their two chicks?" asked Teddy.

"Yup. Dad promised."

"How many days?"

"In six days. The Stoneham Zoo's on the way home."

"We can't forget the peanuts," said Teddy.

"They're in the car."

Abe put his paw on my arm and I scratched his head.

"It's dark," said Teddy. "And the noises outside aren't like at home."

"Insects, I think," I said, although I had no idea what the sounds in the woods were. "Maybe bats."

I lay there in my sleeping bag listening to the creepy forest noises. The ground was hard and there was a rock under my back. I rolled over. The best thing about this trip was thinking about my house back in Somerville waiting for me. Everything was going to feel new when I walked in the door. And I'd decided I was done with perfect Nancy Drew even though I had twenty-eight more in my closet to read. I was going to put them all back in the box and find some books about real kids at the library.

I moved over again trying to get away from the rock.

Camping wasn't exactly what I'd thought it was going to be with the mosquitoes and stinky bathrooms. And if it rained, I wasn't convinced that the canvas tents were going to keep the water out. Now that we'd had the s'mores we should all just head home. But Dad had every day planned. We were going to do all kinds of outdoorsy stuff like fishing in a river, hiking up a mountain, and swimming in a lake. He liked to plan things out and that was okay.

I smiled. The best part of a camping trip was going home. And when I got there I was going to put on some music and maybe I'd dance.

Afterword

Most of the landmarks in Boston, Cambridge, and Somerville, Massachusetts, described in this story do exist. However, Russell Elementary School and some streets in Somerville are fictional.

The parrots Moocher and Minnie lived at the Stoneham Zoo and were later moved to the Franklin Park Zoo in Boston. Moocher was stolen twice but got back home both times. They were rare grand eclectus parrots indigenous to Australia, New Guinea, and many South Pacific Islands. Moocher and Minnie were wonderful parents who raised more than thirty chicks over their long lives in captivity. Many of their offspring now live in zoos all over the world.

The stories and horoscopes Nellie reads all appeared

in the *Boston Herald American* in July 1974. One of those stories turned out to be false. On July 16, 1974, a British doctor claimed that three test-tube babies had been born as a result of his work in perfecting the procedure. Newspapers all over the world published this remarkable story. However, he never provided evidence and most newspapers later corrected their reporting, saying his claim was false. Nellie wouldn't have known this at the time. The first test-tube baby was actually born in 1978. Her name was Louise Brown.

The Watergate investigation went on for over two and a half years. Throughout that period President Nixon tried to stop the investigation. In the end he fought a subpoena from Congress demanding he hand over the remaining secret tape recordings that he had made of conversations in the Oval Office. The Supreme Court ruled 8–0 that he must give investigators the tapes. He finally obeyed the subpoena and released the tapes, which revealed he had obstructed justice and committed other high crimes and misdemeanors. To avoid being impeached and removed from office by Congress, President Nixon resigned on August 9, 1974. His vice president, Gerald Ford, became president the day Nixon resigned.

Mt. Rushmore is located in the Black Hills of South Dakota. Gutzon Borglum and hundreds of stone carvers and laborers worked on the giant presidential heads from 1927 to 1941. In the Treaty of Fort Laramie (1868), the Black Hills were part of the land retained by a number of American Indian tribes. But the United States Congress broke the treaty in 1877 and seized the Black Hills, including the mountain that the Lakota Sioux call the Six Grandfathers (Tunkasila Sakpe). In 1980, the Supreme Court ruled that the US government had taken the Black Hills illegally. The Lakota Sioux refused a financial settlement and continue to demand the return of their land, including the Six Grandfathers, also known as Mt. Rushmore.

Acknowledgments

Many thanks to the travel agents, restaurant workers, bakers, hardware store clerks, and Catholic Church youth educators of Somerville and Cambridge, Massachusetts, with ties to the Azores who told me their stories. The Boston Public Library provided a magnificent setting and knowledgeable research librarians who helped me track down historical details and set me up with microfiche reels of the the *Boston Herald American* circa 1974.

Hugs and thanks to my writer friends who provided support and encouragement—Laura McCaffrey, Tod Olson, Jess Dils, Shelley Tanaka, Sarah Ellis, Margaret Bechard, Julie Larios, and Tomás Kalmar. And thank you to the Loon Song Writer's Retreat for the magic.

I am indebted to my readers—Bridget Kalmar, Mima Tipper, Marion Dane Bauer, Leda Schubert, and Kyle Hiller. Thank you for your wisdom and honesty.

Susan Hawk, thank you for your invaluable feedback on the manuscript and your ongoing support and kindness. I'm so lucky to have you as my agent and my friend.

Thanks to Anna Roberto and the team at Feiwel and Friends at Macmillan for making this book happen. And Ji-Hyuk Kim, thank you for a beautiful cover and the perfect depiction of Abe that graces the start of every chapter.

Much love to my sister Erica and my grandkids, Andrea, Alex, Teddy, and Rosie, and all of my family for their support.

Bridget Kalmar, my sister-in-law and best friend for many decades, you have been my sounding board on our walks in the woods and my first reader. Thank you for your insight, support, and friendship.

And my husband, Georg, who listens to every word of each and every version over and over—your enthusiasm and faith in my work keeps me going. Love and hugs.

THANK YOU FOR READING THIS FEIWEL & FRIENDS BOOK.

The friends who made

STEALING
MT. RUSHMORE

possible are:

Jean Feiwel, Publisher
Liz Szabla, Associate Publisher
Rich Deas, Senior Creative Director
Holly West, Senior Editor
Anna Roberto, Senior Editor
Kat Brzozowski, Senior Editor
Dawn Ryan, Senior Managing Editor
Kim Waymer, Senior Production Manager
Erin Siu, Associate Editor
Emily Settle, Associate Editor
Rachel Diebel, Assistant Editor
Foyinsi Adegbonmire, Editorial Assistant

Follow us on Facebook or visit us online at mackids.com.
Our books are friends for life.

FRIENDS FREE LIBRARY
GERMANTOWN FRIENDS LIBRARY
5418 Germantown Avenue
Philadelphia, PA 19144
215-951-2355

Each borrower is responsible for all items
checked out on his/her library card, for
fines on materials kept overtime, and
replacing any lost or damaged materials.